I0631480

Francis S. Drake

Life and Correspondence of Henry Knox

Major-General in the American Revolutionary Army

Francis S. Drake

Life and Correspondence of Henry Knox
Major-General in the American Revolutionary Army

ISBN/EAN: 9783337227647

Printed in Europe, USA, Canada, Australia, Japan

Cover: Foto ©Andreas Hilbeck / pixelio.de

More available books at **www.hansebooks.com**

LIFE

AND

CORRESPONDENCE

OF

HENRY KNOX,

MAJOR-GENERAL IN THE AMERICAN REVOLUTIONARY
ARMY. -

By FRANCIS S. DRAKE.

——•o✗o•——

BOSTON:
SAMUEL G. DRAKE,
17 BROMFIELD STREET.]
1873.

PREFACE.

THE materials for this Memoir, prepared a short time since for the "Memorials of the Massachusetts Society of the Cincinnati," have been mainly derived from the original letters and papers of General Knox. These papers, which fill fifty-six large portfolios, include, besides Knox's own letters and military papers, many of the letters of Washington, Greene, and other prominent actors in the Revolution and a variety of documents illustrating the history and settlement of that part of Maine included in the Muscongus or Waldo patent. About the year 1840 they were placed by the family in the hands of Hon. Charles S. Daveis of Portland, who began, but did not finish, a memoir of Knox; and in 1853 they were transferred, with the same object, to Mr. Joseph Willard of Boston, a gentleman eminently qualified for the task, but who unfortunately died before its completion. During their transit by water from Portland to Boston, the vessel in which they were embarked was wrecked, and they were slightly injured, having been for some hours submerged. They are now,

LIFE AND CORRESPONDENCE

OF

MAJOR-GENERAL HENRY KNOX.

O F the well-known truth, that Revolutionary epochs
are prolific of great men as well as of exalted ideas,
that period of the history of our own country which marks
its transition from a state of colonial dependence to that
of an independent nation presents a striking example.
Prominent in the remarkable group of which Washington
forms the grand central figure, and second to none in the
esteem, the confidence, and the affection of that illustrious
man, with possibly the single exception of La Fayette,
his adopted son; trusted and leaned upon by him as a
stanch and tried support in moments of anxiety, difficulty, and danger; sharing with him in every conflict
of the Revolution in which that great leader was per-
sonally engaged, — such was Henry Knox, who rose by
the simple force of his character and abilities from the
condition of a volunteer to the highest rank in the army,
that of major-general. Placed at once by his genius
and merit at the head of an important branch of the
military service, — the artillery, — he discovered powers
admirably suited to its requirements, and which cannot
perhaps be better shown than by contrasting the feebleness
and inefficiency of that arm at Bunker's Hill with its terrible efficacy in the trenches of Yorktown.

Inferior, perhaps, as a general to Greene, between whom

and himself the closest ties of friendship existed, he was happier in living to witness the benefits conferred by their toils and sacrifices in the establishment of a constitutional government, a result which, as the head of the war department, he was indefatigable in his efforts to bring about; while under his auspices was achieved also Wayne's memorable victory over the Indians, which gave peace and security to the West, and opened to settlement that immense region destined to be the centre of Western civilization.

While few of our Revolutionary patriots are more worthy of the love and admiration of posterity, there are very few to whose memory so little justice has been accorded. None engaged in the noble cause of freedom with more ardor and enthusiasm; and none with more entire dedication of all the powers of body and mind, both of which were unusually vigorous.

The paternal ancestors of Knox were from the Lowlands of Scotland, a place bearing that name being found on the southern border of the Clyde, within the barony of Renfrew. John Knox, the great reformer, was a native of the neighboring district of East Lothian, where the name is still numerous and respectable. During the reign of James I., many Scotch Presbyterians settled in the north of Ireland, whence numbers of them subsequently emigrated to America, whose descendants were conspicuous in the cause of liberty during the Revolutionary war. In the year 1729 some of these emigrants landed in Boston, bringing with them their pastor, John Morehead, and founded in Bury Street a religious society, which was the origin of the Federal Street Church, afterward the scene of the labors of the eloquent Channing. It is remarkable that the first two names found on the baptismal records of this society, of which the parents of Knox were members, are those of

Knox and Campbell. The tradition in the family of Knox was that they came from the vicinity of Belfast, Ireland, and that William, his father, was a native of St. Eustatia, one of the West Indies. He was married at Boston, on Feb. 11, 1735 (o.s.), by Rev. Mr. Morehead, to Mary, daughter of Robert Campbell; was a ship-master, and the owner of a wharf and a small estate on Sea Street, near Summer,

BIRTHPLACE OF GENERAL KNOX.

which he was in 1756 compelled by misfortune to relinquish, and in 1759 went to St. Eustatia, where he died March 25, 1762, aged fifty years. His widow, Mary, died in Boston, Dec. 14, 1771, aged fifty-three.

Henry, the seventh of ten sons, of whom only four attained to manhood, was born July 25, 1750. His two elder brothers, John and Benjamin, went to sea, and never returned, but were believed to be living in 1769. William, the youngest, born in 1756, some time consul at Dublin, was afterward a clerk in the employ of his brother while Secretary of War, and died insane about the year 1797.

The house in which Knox was born is still standing, and is opposite the head of Drake's Wharf, on Sea Street. It has the gambrel roof common to houses of that period, and was once surrounded by a garden, which has since given place to dwellings. Some changes have taken place in it, as will be observed upon comparing its present appearance with the engraving, which is copied from an old drawing, and preserves its former features. At present a portion of the old house is covered by a modern structure; the doorway has been altered, and a low wooden building intervenes between it and the street. Here the family resided until 1758.

Losing his father about the time when he had completed his grammar-school course, young Knox, upon whom the care of his widowed mother and younger brother now devolved, was fortunate in being employed by Messrs. Wharton & Bowes, booksellers, in Cornhill.*

The excellent Mr. Nicholas Bowes supplied the place of a father to him, keeping a strict eye upon his morals and forming him in early life to habits of industry and regularity. Long afterward he was enabled to repay a portion of his debt to his early benefactor, the widow of Mr. Bowes having become the recipient of his bounty. Among the many estimable traits of Knox's character, that from which in after life he derived the purest satisfaction was the recollection of his attentive and affectionate solicitude for his widowed mother.

Possessing an inquisitive mind and an ardent thirst for knowledge, Knox was not slow in availing himself of the advantages around him for its acquisition, and thus obtained a knowledge of the French language and also of

* In 1761 they took the stock and stand of Daniel Henchman, situated on the south corner of what is now State and Washington Streets. Wharton died about 1768; Bowes, in 1790.

military science, for which he early developed a strong inclination. He was also fond of studying the illustrious examples of antiquity in the pages of Plutarch, and, as Dr. Eliot tells us, "gave early presages of future eminence."

Of a robust and athletic frame, and an enterprising and resolute character, he was foremost in the contests between the North and South Ends, two rival sections of Boston, to the latter of which he belonged; and it is related that once, during the celebration of Pope's Night, the wheel of the carriage which sustained the cumbrous pageant having given way, Knox, to prevent the disgrace sure to result from its non-appearance and the consequent triumph of the adverse party, substituted his own shoulder and bore the vehicle without interruption through the conflict.*

On the evening of the affray of the 5th of March, 1770, which took place in King Street, known as "The Boston Massacre," Knox endeavored to keep the crowd away from the soldiers, and when Captain Preston came upon the ground, " took him by the coat and told him for God's sake to take his men back again, for if they fired his life must answer for the consequence; he replied he was sensible of it, and seemed in great haste and much agitated." Knox saw nothing to justify the use of firearms, and with others remonstrated against the use of them. One result of this lamentable affair was to intensify the hatred of the citizens toward the "bloody backs," as

---

* The 5th of November was set apart for these pageants, which are thus described: An effigy of the Pope and another of the Devil were borne through the streets by a mock procession, and finally were committed to the flames amid the shouts of the surrounding multitude. The rival processions always encountered one another, usually in or about Union Street, and engaged in a pitched battle, ending in the capture of one of the popes and the rout of his supporters, the rival effigies being finally made a bonfire of. The Revolution put an end to these displays.

they styled the red coats, two regiments of whom were upon the demand of the people removed from the town to the castle.

Having attained the age of twenty-one, Knox quitted his employer and began business on his own account. From Edes and Gill's "Gazette" of July 29, 1771, we take the following: "This day is opened a new London Bookstore by HENRY KNOX, opposite Williams' Court in Cornhill, Boston, who has just imported in the last ships from London a large and very elegant assortment of the most modern books in all branches of Literature, Arts, and Sciences, (catalogues of which will be published soon,) and to be sold as cheap as can be bought at any place in town. Also a complete assortment of stationery."

"Knox's Store," says General Henry Burbeck, a contemporary, "was a great resort for the British officers and Tory ladies, who were the *ton* at that period," and Harrison Gray Otis long afterward described it as "one of great display and attraction for young and old, and a fashionable morning lounge." Intelligent, amiable, and patriotic, he was a general favorite, and seemed in a fair way to become a prosperous merchant. The gathering storm of the Revolution, however, loomed dark and threatening in the sky; and ere long the Boston Port Bill, which put a sudden stop to the prosperity of the town, involved also that of our young bookseller.

One of Knox's business correspondents was James Rivington, the Tory bookseller and editor of New York, who sent him (28 July, 1774) five chests of tea, which he understands is very scarce in Boston, and begs him "to put them into such hands in the deepest confidence [this tea had paid no duty, hence the injunction of secrecy], as may be able to complete the sale of them as soon as convenient." Knox declined the commission, and in September Rivington orders its delivery to a Mr. Palfrey.

Rivington, having sent him three hundred " Other Side the Question " (an answer to the " Friendly Address "), under date of 1 Dec. 1774, writes thus : —

" 'The Friendly Address' I do not send to you, for fear of hurting your interest: it was forwarded to Messrs. Mills & Hicks to be printed. My reasons for not troubling you with these very warm, high-seasoned pamphlets is that your very numerous friends on the patriot interest may be greatly disgusted at your distributing them; but if you are not so very nice, as I supposed, from the state of your interest, &c., and are willing to have these sort of articles, I will secure them for you from time to time. Pray explain yourself on this head directly, for I mean to show every expression of my attention to you."

As Knox was thoroughly identified with the ardent sons of liberty, we can easily imagine his reply.

His first purchase of books of Thomas Longman and Sons of London, dated 22 April, 1771, amounted to £340, and up to December, 1772, they had reached a total of £2,066. After this there was a great falling off from political causes, concerning which he writes Longman in November, 1774, as follows : —

" SIR, — I have received yours per Captain Callahan, and the books in good order, also the magazines to August inclusive. I am sorry it is not in my power to make you remittance per this opportunity, but shall do it very soon. This whole continent have entered into a general non-importation agreement until the late acts of parliament respecting this government, &c., are repealed, which will prevent my sending any orders for books until this most desirable end is accomplished. I cannot but hope every person who is concerned in American trade will most strenuously exert themselves, in their respective stations, for what so nearly concerns themselves. I had the fairest prospect of entirely balancing our account this fall;

but the almost total stagnation of trade, in consequence of the Boston Port Bill, has been the sole means of preventing it, and now the non-consumption agreement will stop that small circulation of business left by the Boston Port Bill. I mean the internal business of the province. It must be the wish of every good man that these unhappy differences between Great Britain and the Colonies be speedily and finally adjusted. The influence that the unlucky and unhappy mood of politics of the times has upon trade is my only excuse for writing concerning them. The magazines and new publications concerning the American dispute are the only things which I desire you to send at present."

During the occupancy of the town by the British, and while Knox was with the besieging army, his store, with many others, was robbed and pillaged; and though long after the war he honorably paid Longman a portion of his debt, yet, owing to grave financial embarrassments, a part remained unsettled at his decease. Upon making this last payment of 11,000 guilders (about £1,000), Knox, under date of 15 Dec. 1793, writes thus: —

"It is but justice to myself to say, that while I experience the strongest sensations of gratitude for your forbearance and liberality, that it is with extreme inconvenience that I pay so heavy an arrear for property destroyed by events which I could no more control than I could the great operations of nature, [nor] am I more responsible for them: I mean the war. In paying you, I feel inclination and duty blended together. Had my pecuniary situation admitted of the measure, you should long ago have received the amount due."

At the age of eighteen, Knox, in obedience to a strong natural bent, joined a military company; and when the "Boston Grenadier Corps" was formed by Captain Joseph Peirce, he was one of its founders and was second in command. The splendid uniform, military appearance, drill and efficiency of this corps, which made its first parade June 8, 1772, under Captain Peirce, gave it high renown, and elicited the warm encomiums even of the British officers. Its members, Knox included, had volunteered as a guard over the tea ships; and Governor Gage had been struck by their martial bearing on the occasion of his public entry into Boston in May, 1774. Knox was aided in drilling and disciplining the corps by its orderly sergeant, Lemuel Trescott, afterward a major, and one of the best officers in the Continental Army; and each man was from five feet ten to six feet in height. By conversing with the British officers who frequented his bookstore, by earnest study of military authors and by careful observation of the soldiery in Boston, he soon attained great proficiency in the theory and practice of the military art.

While on a gunning excursion among the islands in Boston harbor (24 July, 1773), he lost, by the bursting of his fowling-piece, the two smaller fingers of his left hand, a defect he was accustomed to cover up by the folds of a handkerchief, and which, in Stuart's half-length portrait in Faneuil Hall, is skilfully concealed by resting the hand on a cannon.*

It was about a month after this occurrence that Knox, who was an uncommonly good-looking officer, and possessed also a fine military bearing, attracted the attention of his future wife. This is related, on the authority of General Burbeck, as having taken place " at the next parade of the corps, when Lieutenant Knox appeared with the wound handsomely bandaged with a scarf, which of course

* Other portraits of Knox are that by C. W. Peale and the one by Edward Savage, from which the engraving accompanying this volume is taken. Concerning this picture, Savage writes to Knox from London, Jan. 22, 1792 : —

"Agreeable to your request, I have sent by Mr. West the half-dozen prints from the original portrait which you did me the honor to sit for. . . . I was much flattered by Mr. West, historical painter to his Majesty, as he knew it to be my first performance on copper, and without any assistance.

" No. 29 CHARLES STREET, Middlesex Hospital."

excited the sympathy of all the ladies." The good impression thus made was improved by the young lady's visits to his bookstore, and an acquaintance soon sprung up, which ripened into mutual love and esteem, and resulted in a true and happy union.* Her father, Thomas Flucker, Esq., "a high-toned loyalist, of great family pretensions," and Secretary of the Province of Massachusetts Bay, was exceedingly averse to the match, as indeed were all of the young lady's aristocratic connections, who were Tories, while Knox's sympathies were, as was well known, strongly enlisted in behalf of his countrymen. Indeed, the match is said to have wanted little of an elopement on this account, her friends regarding her social prospects as ruined by her wedding one who had embraced the rebel cause.

The consequences were depicted to her in lively colors, and without any softening of the shades. She was told that, while her sisters were riding in their coaches, she would be eating the bread of poverty and dependence; that there could be but one issue to the conflict; and that the power of Great Britain was overwhelming. Disregarding all these well-meant warnings, the young lady, who had fully adopted the views and feelings of her future husband, resolved to follow the fortunes of him to whom her heart had been given. Here is a brief glimpse of their courtship : —

KNOX TO MISS FLUCKER.

"Monday Evening, March 7, 1774.

" What news? Have you spoken to your father, or he to you, upon the subject? What appearance has this [to us] grand affair

---

* Mr. Otis, whom we have before quoted, says : " Miss Flucker was distinguished as a young lady of high intellectual endowments, very fond of books, and especially the books sold by Knox, to whose shelves she had frequent recourse."

at your house at present? Do you go to the ball to-morrow evening? I am in a state of anxiety heretofore unknown. I wish the medium of our correspondence settled, in order to which I must endeavor to see you, when we will settle it."

Love, as usual, triumphed over all obstacles; and in the "Gazette" of June 20, 1774, the marriage was thus announced: —

"Last Thursday (the 16th), was married, by the Rev. Dr. Caner, Mr. Henry Knox of this town, to Miss Lucy Flucker, second daughter to the Hon. Thomas Flucker, Esq., Secretary of the Province."

The young couple at once commenced housekeeping, but their domestic enjoyments were seriously interrupted by the events of the 19th of April, 1775; and just one year from the day of his marriage Knox quitted Boston in disguise (his departure having been interdicted by Gage), accompanied by his wife, who had quilted into the lining of her cloak the sword with which her husband was to carve out a successful military career. Large promises had been held out to Knox to induce him to follow the royal standard, as it was thought of consequence to prevent so talented a young man from attaching himself to the provincials; but his patriotism was as sincere as it was ardent, and he did not for a moment hesitate, but embarked heart and hand in the patriot cause.

Repairing at once to the head-quarters of General Ward at Cambridge, he was actively engaged in reconnoitring service on the memorable 17th of June, and upon his reports the general's orders were issued. After the battle, his wife having been safely bestowed at Worcester, Knox, while declining any particular commission, lent his aid in planning and constructing works of defence for the various camps around the beleaguered town, at the same time acquiring skill as an artillerist, and was thus occupied for

some months. In this employment, the comparative proficiency he had acquired, by seizing every chance occasion
for mastering that branch of military science, was of sensible service to his country, then greatly in need of skilled
engineers; and it also proved the stepping-stone to his
future distinction. The chief work constructed by him
was the strong redoubt crowning the hill in Roxbury,
known as Roxbury Fort, the site of which is now covered
by the Cochituate Stand Pipe. A few extracts from his
letters to his wife and to his brother during the siege are
here given, from the first of which it appears that his
skill and activity had attracted the notice of Washington
only three days after he had taken the command of the
army: —

"ROXBURY (Lemuel Childs's),
"Thursday Morning, 6 o'clock (July 6, 1775).

"Yesterday, as I was going to Cambridge, I met the generals
[Washington and Lee], who begged me to return to Roxbury again,
which I did. When they had viewed the works, they expressed the
greatest pleasure and surprise at their situation and apparent utility,
to say nothing of the plan, which did not escape their praise."

"WATERTOWN, July 9.

"General Washington fills his place with vast ease and dignity,
and dispenses happiness around him. General Lee will become
very popular soon. I am obliged to go to Cambridge to wait on
General Washington, and promised to be there by seven o'clock. I
am now half past that time."

"Monday, July 11.

"I go to Roxbury and Cambridge in the morning, and return
here every evening for the sake of Mr. Jackson's company. We
are here in a very decent private house, — Mr. Cook's, near the
bridge. . . . You heard, I suppose, by our neighbor Curtis that our
people burnt Brown's houses on Boston Neck, except the store? It
was a brave action, and well performed. The regulars were in
such trepidation in Boston and on the lines that I perfectly believe
750 men would at that time [have] taken the full possession of the

town. The new generals are of infinite service in the army. They have to reduce order almost from a perfect chaos. I think they are in a fair way of doing it. Our army still 'affect to hold the army besieged,'* and will effectually continue to do so."

> "August 9, 1775
> "(General Thomas's Head-quarters, Roxbury).

"I was yesterday at Cambridge. Generals Washington and Lee inquired after you. I dined at General W.'s. While I was there, the navy prisoners whom I wrote to you about yesterday came there on horses. There were seven; viz., one lieutenant,† one doctor, one master, and four midshipmen,—all handsome, genteel-looking men. The officers were disposed of genteelly for the present, and are soon to be sent into the country."

To his brother William, 25 Sept. 1775: —

"Last Friday Lucy [Mrs. Knox] dined at General Washington's. Last Saturday, let it be remembered to the honor and skill of the British troops, that they fired 104 cannon-shot at [our] works, at not a greater distance than half point blank shot,—and did what? Why, scratched a man's face with the splinters of a rail-fence! I have had the pleasure of dodging these heretofore engines of terror with great success; nor am I afraid they will [hit me?], unless directed by the hand of Providence."

On page eighty-six of John Adams's autobiography, he says: "Colonel Knox had been a youth who had attracted my notice by his pleasing manners and inquisitive turn of mind, when I was a man in business in Boston;" and on the same day (Oct. 1, 1776) he writes to Knox, requesting his sentiments upon a plan for the establishment of a military academy in the army. The following letter, writ-

---

* A phrase in Gage's irate proclamation of June 12, which caused much merriment in the American camp.

† John Knight, afterward an admiral. They were taken at Machias; and the question as to the treatment to be accorded them led to the memorable correspondence upon the subject between Washington and the British commander, Gage.

ten while in attendance upon Congress, still further evinces
Mr. Adams's appreciation of him: —

JOHN ADAMS TO KNOX.

"PHILADELPHIA, Nov. 11, 1775.

"I had the pleasure of a letter from you a few days ago, and was
rejoiced to learn that you have at last determined to take a more
important share than you have done hitherto in the conduct of our
military matters. I have been impressed with an opinion of your
knowledge and abilities in the military way for several years, and of
late have endeavored, both at camp, at Watertown, and at Philadelphia, by mentioning your name and character, to make you more
known, and consequently in a better way for promotion.

"It was a sincere opinion of your merit and qualifications which
prompted me to act this part, and therefore I am very happy to be
able to inform you that I believe you will very soon be provided for
according to your wishes; at least you may depend upon this, that
nothing in my power shall be wanting to effect it. It is of vast
importance, my dear sir, that I should be minutely informed of every
thing which passes at the camp while I hold a place in the great
Council of America; and therefore I must beg the favor of you to
write me as often as you can by safe conveyances. I want to know
the name, rank, and character of every officer in the army, — I
mean every honest and able one; but more especially of every
officer who is best acquainted with the theory and practice of forti-
fication and gunnery. What is comprehended within the term
Engineer? and whether it includes skill both in fortifications and
gunnery; and what skilful engineers you have in the army; and
whether any of them, and who, have seen service, and when and
where.

"I want to know if there is a complete set of books upon the
military art in all its branches in the library of Harvard College,
and what books are the best upon those subjects."

On Nov. 2, Washington writes to Governor Trumbull
respecting the want of competent engineers, and says:
"Most of the works which have been thrown up for the
defence of our several encampments have been planned

by a few of the principal officers of the army, assisted by
Mr. Knox, a gentleman of Worcester."

And to the President of Congress on the 8th of the
same month: —

"The council of officers are unanimously of opinion that the command of the artillery should no longer continue in Colonel Gridley;
and knowing of no person better qualified to supply his place, or
whose appointment will give more general satisfaction, I have taken
the liberty of recommending Henry Knox to the consideration of
Congress."

Gridley, a veteran of the French war, was incapacitated
by age and infirmity for active service; and the next in
rank, David Mason, offered to serve as lieutenant-colonel
of the artillery regiment if Knox might be appointed
colonel. There were a number of young officers of merit
in that branch,* but they joined unanimously in making
this request; and he was accordingly commissioned by
Congress colonel of the artillery regiment on Nov. 17,
1775. His commission did not reach him, however, until
after his return from Ticonderoga.†

The want of heavy ordnance, with which to drive the·

---

* Many of these officers, among whom were John Crane, Ebenezer Stevens,
Winthrop Sargent, and others, who became distinguished, were trained in
Paddock's artillery company, formed in 1763 by David Mason. Paddock,
who succeeded him in the command in 1768, brought it to a high state of
efficiency; but being a Tory left Boston with the British troops, and died in
the Isle of Jersey, 25 March, 1804, aged seventy-six.

† It seems not a little singular that one who had never been even a private
of artillery, nor had the advantages of a military school, should have been
selected for the eminently practical rôle of chief of artillery of the army. His
fitness for the position was, however, conceded at once and without question,
and was afterward abundantly manifested.

A return of the artillery regiment, consisting of twelve companies, dated
3 March, 1776, gives 635 men. The field-officers were — Henry Knox,
colonel; William Burbeck, first lieutenant-colonel; David Mason, second
lieutenant-colonel; John Crane, first major; John Lamb, second major.

4

enemy from Boston, was felt to be one of serious concern; and to the enterprising and fertile mind of Knox belongs the credit of having conceived and successfully executed a project by which the besieging army was supplied with the means for effecting that important object. This plan, which was approved by Washington, was to procure from Fort Ticonderoga the needed cannon and stores, and to transport them on boats and sleds to the camp at Cambridge.

Armed with the necessary instructions from the commander-in-chief, and accompanied by his younger brother, William, then nineteen years of age, and who was of great service to him in this enterprise, Knox left the camp at Cambridge on Nov. 15, and, after a brief visit to his wife at Worcester, reached New York on the 25th. After transacting his business there, he started northward on the 28th, "glad," as he writes in his diary, "to leave New York, it being very expensive." He reached Albany Dec. 1, and Ticonderoga on the 5th. From this place he began his laborious and difficult journey homeward on the 9th, having put on board some small craft, such ordnance and stores as were essential and could be safely transported. He was assisted in his arduous labors by General Schuyler, and after undergoing much hardship and suffering, and encountering numerous obstacles as well as the annoyances and vexations incident to so hazardous an enterprise in the midst of a severe winter, he finally had the satisfaction of reaching camp on Jan. 24, 1776, and of receiving the congratulations of the commander-in-chief upon the important service he had thus rendered the army and the country. While crossing the Hudson on the ice, one of the cannon fell into the river near the landing. It was recovered on the following day, with the assistance of the people of Albany, in return for which service Knox christened her "The Albany."

This achievement stamped the character of Knox for boldness, enterprise, fertility of resource and genius, supplied the means for fortifying Dorchester Heights, and vindicated the judgment of Washington in selecting him for the important and responsible duties of the artillery and ordnance departments.*

A memorable incident of this journey was his encounter with the gallant but unfortunate André. The latter, who had been taken prisoner by Montgomery at St. John's, was on his way to Lancaster, Pa., to remain there until exchanged, while Knox was pursuing his way northward. Chance made them one stormy winter night inmates of the same cabin on the border of Lake George, and even of the same bed. Though of opposite political attachments, they had much in common. Their ages were alike; each had given up the pursuits of trade for the military profession, of which each had made a study; and their tastes and aims were similar. They parted on the morrow with strong mutual sentiments of regard and good-will, and their interview left an indelible impression on the mind of Knox. The respective condition of the two was not mutually made known until just as they were about to part; and when Knox, a few years later, was called on to perform the painful office of a judge upon that tribunal which condemned André to death, the memory of their meeting gave additional bitterness to that unpleasant duty.

To Washington he wrote on Nov. 27, from New York, earnestly recommending that cannon for the army be cast there, " where it can be expeditiously and cheaply done."

---

* "For expenditures in a journey from the camp round Boston to New York, Albany, and Ticonderoga, and from thence, with 55 pieces of iron and brass ordnance, 1 barrel of flints, and 23 boxes of lead, back to camp (including expenses of self, brother, and servant), £520.15.8¾." — *Knox's Account-book.* (For schedule of cannon, &c., see Appendix.)

And on Dec. 17, from Fort George : —

" I returned to this place on the 15th, and brought with me the
cannon, it being nearly the time I computed it would take us to
transport them here. It is not easy to conceive the difficulties we
have had in getting them over the lake, owing to the advanced
season of the year and contrary winds; but the danger is now past.
Three days ago it was very uncertain whether we should have
gotten them until next spring; but now, please God, they must go.
I have had made 42 exceeding strong sleds, and have provided
80 yoke of oxen to drag them as far as Springfield, where I shall
get fresh cattle to carry them to camp. The route will be from here
to Kinderhook, from thence to Great Barrington, and down to
Springfield. I have sent for the sleds and teams to come here, and
expect to begin to move them to Saratoga on Wednesday or Thursday next, trusting that between this and then we shall have a fine
fall of snow, which will enable us to proceed further, and make the
carriage easy. If that shall be the case, I hope in sixteen or seventeen days' time to be able to present to your Excellency a noble
train of artillery."

From Albany, 5th Jan. 1776 : —

" I was in hopes that we should have been able to have had the
cannon at Cambridge by this time. The want of snow detained us
some days, and now a cruel thaw hinders from crossing Hudson
River, which we are obliged to do four times from Lake George to
this town. The first severe night will make the ice on the river
sufficiently strong; till that happens the cannon and mortars must
remain where they are. These inevitable delays pain me exceedingly, as my mind is fully sensible of the importance of the greatest
expedition in this case. . . . General Schuyler has been exceedingly
assiduous in this matter. As to myself, my utmost endeavors have
been, and still shall be, used to forward them with the utmost despatch."

And on the same day he writes to his wife : —

" . . . A little about my travels. New York is a place where I
think in general the houses are better built than in Boston. They
are generally of brick, and three stories high, with the largest kind

of windows. Their churches are grand; their college, workhouse, and hospitals most excellently situated, and also exceedingly commodious; their principal streets much wider than ours. The people,—why, the people are magnificent: in their equipages, which are numerous; in their house furniture, which is fine; in their pride and conceit, which are inimitable; in their profaneness, which is intolerable; in the want of principle, which is prevalent; in their Toryism, which is unsufferable, and for which they must repent in dust and ashes. The country from New York to this city [Albany] is not very populous,—not the fifth part so much so as in New England, and with much greater marks of poverty than there. The people of this city, of which there are about 5,000 or 6,000, are, I believe, honest enough, and many of them sensible people,— much more so than any other part of the government which I've seen. There are four very good buildings for public worship, with a State House, the remains of capital barracks, hospital, and fort, which must in their day have been very clever. (It is situated on the side of a hill.)

"Albany, from its situation, and commanding the trade of the water and the immense territories westward, must one day be, if not the capital, yet nearly to it, of America. There are a number of gentlemen's very elegant seats in view from that part of the river before the town, among them I think General Schuyler's claims the preference; the owner of which is sensible and polite, and I think has behaved with vast propriety to the British officers who, by the course of war, have fallen into our hands. Certain of them set out from this for Pennsylvania yesterday, among whom was General Prescott, who has by all accounts behaved exceedingly ill to Colonel Allen of ours, who was taken at Montreal. Here is also Major Gamble, who wrote the letters from Quebec which were published last summer. There are in all about sixty commissioned officers, besides about twenty of the Canadian noblesse, who appeared as lively and happy as if nothing [had] happened. One or two of the officers I pitied, the others seemed concerned, but not humbled. The women and children suffer amazingly at this advanced season of the year. It is now past twelve o'clock, therefore I wish you a good night's repose, and will mention you in my prayers."

On the night of the 4th of March, 1776, under cover of a furious cannonade from Knox's batteries at Cobble Hill,

Lechmere's Point, and Roxbury, General Thomas took possession of Dorchester Heights commanding the town and harbor of Boston, which he so strongly fortified that Howe, the British commander, though he made preparations to attack him on the following day, dared not do so, and was consequently obliged to evacuate Boston on the 17th.*

Reinforcements were immediately sent to the northern army ; and the remainder of Washington's force was, early in April, moved to New York, which was soon to become the theatre of active operations.

Knox's engineering talents were now called into requisition in Connecticut and Rhode Island ; and previous to his arrival in New York, on the 30th of April, he wrote to Washington and to Mrs. Knox several letters, from which we extract as follows : —

TO WASHINGTON.

"NORWICH, 21 April, 1776.

" In passing through Providence, Governor Cooke and a number of the principal people were very pressing for me to take Newport in my way, in order to mark out some works of defence for that place. The spirited conduct of the colony troops posted there, in driving away the king's ships, alarmed the whole colony for the safety of its capital. Knowing your Excellency's anxiety for the preservation of every part of the continent, I conceived it to be my duty to act in conformity to your wishes, especially as I could get to Norwich as soon as the stores which set out on the 14th. Accordingly I went to Newport, and marked out five batteries, which, from the advantageous situation of the ground, must, when executed, render the harbor exceedingly secure.

" Lieutenant-Colonel Burbeck declined complying with your Excellency's orders, alleging that the province had settled on him four shillings sterling per day during life, after the war was over, which, if

---

* The Fluckers accompanied the royal troops to Halifax, and sailed thence to England, where the father and mother of Mrs. Knox both died : the former, in March, 1783 ; the latter, in December, 1785.

he went out of the province, he might perhaps lose.* Lieutenant-
Colonel Mason, who came with the ordnance to this town, being in
ill health, I have permitted to go by land."

TO WASHINGTON.

"NEW LONDON, April 24, 1776.

"SIR,—In consequence of your Excellency's directions, I am
employed in looking at and getting the necessary information respecting the harbor, in which I shall spare no pains. I mentioned
to your Excellency Newport harbor, which, in conjunction with
this, will, when fortified, afford a safe retreat to the American navy
or their prizes in any wind that blows. They are equally convenient for ships coming from sea; and if the wind is not fair to go
into one harbor, they may go into the other. The artillery and
stores are all embarked, together with the remaining company of
my regiment, and have been waiting for a fair wind two days.

"Admiral Hopkins is still in this harbor, and I believe will be
obliged to continue here some time. He has this day received intelligence that four ships and two brigs are off Montauk Point and
Rhode Island, stationed in such a manner that but one appears at a
time, and each able to come up to the assistance of the others. The
captain of the 'Cerberus' was on Block Island yesterday, and told a
man there that he was waiting for Admiral Hopkins, and expected
in four days to be joined by Captain Wallace and his squadron."

In a letter to his wife he thus describes Admiral
Hopkins:—

"I have been on board Admiral Hopkins's [ship], and in company
with his gallant son who was wounded in the engagement with the
'Glasgow.' The admiral is an antiquated figure. He brought to
my mind Van Tromp, the famous Dutch admiral. Though antiquated in figure, he is shrewd and sensible. I, whom you think
not a little enthusiastic, should have taken him for an angel, only he
swore now and then."

* This officer remained in Massachusetts and never rejoined the regiment.
He was many years commander at Castle William, and died in Boston, 22 July,
1785, aged sixty-nine.

To protect New York city, Washington was compelled to hold Kingsbridge, Governor's Island, Paulus Hook, and the Heights of Brooklyn. For all these posts, separated by water, some of them fifteen miles apart, he had, early in August, but about 10,000 men fit for duty, beside Knox's regiment of artillery. Most of the cannon in the field-works were of iron, old and honey-combed, broken and defective.*

On July 11th Knox writes to his brother: —

" DEAR BILLY,—I received your affectionate letter by the post, for which I thank you. In consequence of a false report, my Lucy and her babe are at Stamford or Fairfield, where she writes me she is very unhappy, and wants to return here again, which would make me as unhappy in contemplating the idea which you had of her flight as if it was real. Indeed, the circumstances of our parting were extremely disagreeable. She had, contrary to my opinion, stayed too long. From the hall window, where we usually break-fasted, we saw the ships coming through the Narrows, with a fair wind and rapid tide, which would have brought them up to the city in about half an hour. You can scarcely conceive the distress and anxiety that she then had. The city in an uproar, the alarm guns firing, the troops repairing to their posts, and every thing in the [height] of bustle; I not at liberty to attend her, as my country calls loudest. My God, may I never experience the like feelings again! They were too much; but I found a way to disguise them, for I scolded like a fury at her for not having gone before."

To Mrs. Knox, at Norwalk or Fairfield, 13th July: —

" I thank heaven you were not here yesterday. Two ships and three tenders of the enemy about twenty minutes past three weighed anchor, and in twenty-five minutes were before the town. We had a

---

* On June 10, Knox reported to Washington that there were mounted, and fit for action in the city and neighboring posts, 121 heavy and light cannon, requiring for their service 1,210 men. His regiment, present and fit for duty, numbered (including 50 officers) 520. He therefore recommends that it be immediately raised to the required number by draught from the other battalions.

loud cannonade, but could not stop them, though I believe we damaged them much. They kept over on the Jersey side too far from our batteries. I was so unfortunate as to lose six men by accidents, and a number wounded. This affair will be of service to my people: it will teach them to moderate their fiery courage."

August 11th, he again writes her: —

"You wish to know how I pass my time. I generally rise with or a little before the sun, and immediately with a part of the regiment attend prayers, sing a psalm, and read a chapter in [the Bible at] the Grand Battery. General Putnam constantly attends. I despatch a considerable deal of business before breakfast. From breakfast to dinner I am broiling in a sun hot enough to roast an egg. Sometimes I dine with the generals, Washington, Putnam, Stirling, &c.; but I am mortified that I haven't had them to dine with me in return. However, that cannot be. I go to bed at nine o'clock or before, every night."

Knox's quarters were at the battery near those of Washington, with whom he crossed over to Long Island daily, in the discharge of his duty. He thus writes to his wife of the disaster of Aug. 27th: —

"About two o'clock in the morning (yesterday) the enemy attacked the woods in front of our works on Long Island, where our riflemen lay. They attacked with a chosen part of the Hessians, and all the light infantry and grenadiers of the army, and after about six or seven hours' smart skirmishing our people fell back in front of our works. The enemy lost nearly one thousand killed. We lost about the same number killed, wounded, and taken prisoners, among whom are General Sullivan and Lord Stirling. General Parsons was missing until this morning, when he returned. I met with some loss in my regiment: they behaved like heroes, and are gone to glory. I was not on the island myself, being obliged to wait on my Lord Howe and the navy gentry who threatened to pay us a visit."

To the same Sept. 5th: —

"We want great men, who when fortune frowns will not be discouraged. God will I trust in time give us these men. The Congress will ruin every thing by their stupid parsimony, and they begin to see it. It is, as I always said, misfortunes that must raise us to the character of a *great people*. One or two drubbings will be of service to us; and one severe defeat to the enemy, ruin. We must have a standing army. The militia get sick, or think themselves so, and run home ; and wherever they go, they spread a panic."

On the 15th of September the army of General Howe effected a landing at Kip's Bay, about three miles above the city, the evacuation of which, already in progress, was hurriedly completed by the Americans. Knox, who had for some days been engaged in removing the ordnance and stores, left the city about twelve o'clock to join General Washington. Encountering Silliman's brigade, retreating in great confusion in the vicinity of Corlaer's Hook, he lost time in attempting to rally the fugitives, with whom he then threw himself into Fort Bunker Hill, an unfinished work near the site of the present Centre Market, where he "thought only of a gallant defence." Colonel Aaron Burr, who was one of Putnam's aids, riding up, assured the troops that a retreat was practicable, and led them in safety to the Bloomingdale road, near what is now 60th Street. Knox, who was almost the last to leave the city, escaped capture only by seizing a boat and making his way by water. His arrival at Harlem, where great anxiety was felt for his safety, was greeted with a shout of welcome, and by an embrace from Washington.

To his brother he writes on the 19th: "My constant fatigue and application to the business of my extensive department has been such that I have not had my

clothes off once o' nights for more than forty days."
And again : —

"HEIGHTS OF HARLEM, 8 miles from New York,
Sept. 23d.

"You, with our other friends at Boston, are anxious for our situation and wish to know it exactly. It is my lot, and it has been
so invariably since I have been in the army, to be in an exceeding
busy department. This I mention not by way of dislike, but as
an excuse for any seeming negligence or remissness in writing to
you. . . . The general leading features or outlines of what has already
happened have, almost ever since I have been this way, been fully
impressed on my mind. Islands separated from the main by nav-
igable waters are not to be defended by a people without a navy
against a nation who can send a powerful fleet to interrupt the communication. We had one chance to defend New York. I don't
know whether to call it a whole chance. I think I cannot with
propriety : it was only part of a chance, which was by being completely victorious on Long Island. Even had this event taken place,
they could have burnt the town by their shipping : this is indisputable, in my opinion. They in their first attack on Long Island,
lost us by our own fault in not guarding the passes, made such
lodgement near our works, that they were not obliged to leave more
than five thousand men to guard them. This would have left fifteen
thousand men at least to have made a push up the North River,
and landed in our rear and fortified. Had they taken this measure,
which in good policy they ought to have done, they might at one
stroke have reduced the whole army to the necessity of becoming
prisoners without being able to fight in the least. But in this and
several other capital matters they have not acted the great war-
riors : indeed I see nothing of the *vast* about them either in their
designs or execution. But, good God, if they are little, thou
knowest full well we are much less, and that nothing less than the
infatuation of the enemy and the almost immediate interposition
of thy providence has saved this rabble army.

" The general is as worthy a man as breathes, but he cannot do
every thing nor be everywhere. He wants good assistants. There
is a radical evil in our army, — the lack of officers. We ought to
have men of merit in the most extensive and unlimited sense of
the word. Instead of which, the bulk of the officers of the army

are a parcel of ignorant, stupid men, who might make tolerable soldiers, but [are] bad officers; and until Congress forms an establishment to induce men proper for the purpose to leave their usual employments and enter the service, it is ten to one they will be beat till they are heartily tired of it. We ought to have academies, in which the whole theory of the art of war shall be taught, and every other encouragement possible given to draw persons into the army that may give a lustre to our arms. As the army now stands, it is only a receptacle for ragmuffins. You will observe I am chagrined, not more so than at any other time since I've been in the army; but many late affairs, of which I've been an eye-witness, have so totally sickened me, that unless some very different mode of conduct is observed in the formation of the new army, I shall not think myself obliged by either the laws of God or nature to risk my reputation on so cobweb a foundation.

"The affair of last Monday (battle of Harlem Plains) has had some good consequences towards raising the people's spirits. They find that if they stick to these mighty men they will run as fast as other people. We pursued them nearly two miles. About fifteen hundred of our troops engaged; of the enemy, about the same number. The grounds on which we now rest are strong, I think we shall defend them: if we don't, I hope God will punish us both in this world and the world to come, if the fault is ours. Pay Mrs. Crane, wife to Major Crane, fifty dollars, and inform her that the Major is in a fair way to do well. He is in high esteem in the army, and the loss of his services much regretted by me.* The

---

* Crane had, a few days before, been wounded in the foot by a shot from Captain Wallace's frigate, which he was cannonading. John Crane was born at Braintree, Mass., 7 December, 1744, and died at Whiting, Me., 21 August, 1805. He was a housewright; was one of the "Tea Party," and lived in a house still standing in Tremont Street, Boston, opposite Hollis Street. He removed to Providence in 1774, and there raised a company of artillery, with which he joined Gridley's regiment in the summer of 1775, with the rank of major. He received the same commission in Knox's regiment, Jan. 1, 1776, and raised in the following year and commanded throughout the war a regiment of continental artillery. Colonel Crane was one of the members of Paddock's artillery company before the war, and distinguished himself upon several occasions during the contest, being honorably mentioned by General Sullivan during the Rhode Island expedition. After the war he carried on the lumber business in Washington County, Me.

scoundrel Hessians took my baggage-cart, with the great part of my necessary matters, which I find very difficult to replace at present."

He writes him also an account of the action of Oct. 28th : —

"Near WHITE PLAINS, 32 miles from New York,
1 Nov. 1776.

"Last Monday, the enemy with nearly their whole force advanced upon the hills above us; and soon after ten o'clock in the morning, with a large part of their army, began a most furious attack on a hill (Chatterton's) on our right, where we had about one thousand posted under General McDougall, which they carried with considerable loss. Our loss was not very great. Our men had no works, and were not timely reinforced, owing to the distance they were from the main body. The enemy's having possession of this hill obliged us to abandon some slight lines thrown up on White Plains. This we did this morning, and retired to some hills about half a mile in the rear. The enemy are determined on something decisive, and we are determined to risk a general battle only on the most advantageous terms. We are manœuvring, in which I think they are somewhat our superiors."

The loss of Fort Washington, which took place on Nov. 16th, was a serious blow to the Americans. General Greene's mortification at the event, as well as his reasons for endeavoring to hold that post, are given for the first time in this highly interesting letter to his friend Knox: —

"FORT LEE, Nov. [17], 1776.

"Your favor of the 14th reached me in a melancholy temper. The misfortune of losing Fort Washington, with between two and three thousand men, will reach you before this, if it has not already. His Excellency General Washington has been with me for several days. The evacuation or reinforcement of Fort Washington was under consideration, but finally nothing concluded on. Day before yesterday, about one o'clock, Howe's adjutant-general made a demand of the surrender of the garrison in the general's name, but was answered by the commanding officer that he should defend it to the last extremity. Yesterday morning, General Washington, General Putnam, General Mercer, and myself went to the island to determine what was best to be done; but just at the instant we stepped on board the boat the enemy made their appearance on the hill where the Monday action was, and began a severe cannonade with several field-pieces. Our guards soon fled, the enemy advanced up to the second line. This was done while we were crossing the river and getting upon the hill. The enemy made several marches to the right and to the left, — I suppose to reconnoitre the fortifications and lines.

There we all stood in a very awkward situation. As the disposition was made, and the enemy advancing, we durst not attempt to make any new disposition; indeed, we saw nothing amiss. We all urged his Excellency to come off. I offered to stay, General Putnam did the same, and so did General Mercer; but his Excellency thought it best for us all to come off together, which we did, about half an hour before the enemy surrounded the fort. The enemy came up Harlem River, and landed a party at head-quarters, which was upon the back of our people in the lines. A disorderly retreat soon took place; without much firing the people retreated into the fort. On the north side of the fort there was a very heavy fire for a long while; and as they had the advantage of the ground, I apprehend the enemy's loss must be great. After the troops retreated in the fort, very few guns were fired. The enemy approached within small-arm fire of the lines, and sent in a flag, and the garrison capitulated in an hour. I was afraid of the fort: the redoubt you and I advised, too, was not done, or little or nothing done to it. Had that been complete, I think the garrison might have defended themselves a long while, or been brought off. I feel mad, vexed, sick, and sorry. Never did I need the consoling voice of a friend more than now. Happy should I be to see you. This is a most terrible event: its consequences are justly to be dreaded. Pray, what is said upon the occasion? A line from you will be very acceptable.

I am, dear sir, your obedient servant,   N. GREENE.

" No particulars of the action as yet has come to my knowledge. [Mem. on the back.] I have not time to give you a description of the battle.

[Addressed:]
To Coll° HENRY KNOX,
      White Plains.

In this unfortunate affair, the artillery regiment lost about one hundred men, including Captain Pierce. Then followed the evacuation of Fort Lee and the memorable retreat of Washington's little army through the Jerseys, "protracted for eighteen or nineteen days in an inclement season, often in sight and within cannon-shot of his enemies, his rear pulling down bridges and their van building them up," delaying them till midwinter and impassable roads should close the campaign. On Dec. 13th, Howe, believing that the American force would melt away at the near expiration of their engagements, returned to his winter quarters in New York, leaving Colonel Donop with his Hessians and the 42d Highlanders to hold the line from Trenton to Burlington.

At this critical moment, when even the calm soul of Washington trembled for his country's freedom, Knox was one of those who strengthened his hand and encouraged his heart; and his letters written in the darkest periods of the war show that he never yielded to despondency, but confidently anticipated its triumphant issue.

Washington now resolved to strike a blow that should cripple his enemy and revive the sinking spirit of his countrymen. He crossed the Delaware, Knox superintending its passage, and by his stentorian voice making audible the orders of his chief above the fury of the blast, and surprising the post at Trenton captured the entire garrison. After this victory, Knox and Greene were in favor of following it up by marching upon New Brunswick. Washington was inclined to adopt this course, but the generality of the other officers opposed it, an opposition they afterward regretted. His account of this and the subsequent brilliant affair at Princeton is given in the following letters to Mrs. Knox: —

"DELAWARE RIVER, near TRENTON,
Dec. 28, 1776, near 12 o'clock.

"MY DEARLY BELOVED FRIEND,—You will before this have heard of our success on the morning of the 26th instant. The enemy, by their superior marching, had obliged us to retire on the Pennsylvania side of the Delaware, by which means we were obliged to evacuate or give up nearly all the Jerseys. Soon after our retiring over the river, the preservation of Philadelphia was a matter exceedingly precarious,—the force of the enemy three or four times as large as ours. However, they seemed content with their success for the present, and quartered their troops in different and distant places in the Jerseys. Of these cantonments Trenton was the most considerable.

"Trenton is an open town, situated nearly on the banks of the Delaware, accessible on all sides. Our army was scattered along the river for nearly twenty-five miles. Our intelligence agreed that the force of the enemy in Trenton was from two to three thousand, with about six field cannon, and that they were pretty secure in their situation, and that they were Hessians,—no British troops. A hardy design was formed of attacking the town by storm. Accordingly a part of the army, consisting of about 2,500 or 3,000, passed the river on Christmas night, with almost infinite difficulty, with eighteen field-pieces. The floating ice in the river made the labor almost incredible. However, perseverance accomplished what at first seemed impossible. About two o'clock the troops were all on the Jersey side; we then were about nine miles from the object. The night was cold and stormy; it hailed with great violence; the troops marched with the most profound silence and good order.

"They arrived by two routes at the same time, about half an hour after daylight, within one mile of the town. The storm continued with great violence, but was in our backs, and consequently in the faces of our enemy. About half a mile from the town was an advanced guard on each road, consisting of a captain's guard. These we forced, and entered the town with them pell-mell; and here succeeded a scene of war of which I had often conceived, but never saw before. The hurry, fright, and confusion of the enemy was [not] unlike that which will be when the last trump shall sound. They endeavored to form in streets, the heads of which we had previously the possession of with cannon and howitzers; these, in the twinkling of an eye, cleared the streets. The backs of the houses were resorted to for shelter. These proved ineffectual: the musketry soon dislodged them. Finally they were driven through the town into an open plain beyond. Here they formed in an instant. During the contest in the streets measures were taken for putting an entire stop to their retreat by posting troops and cannon in such passes and roads as it was possible for them to get away by. The poor fellows after they were formed on the plain saw themselves completely surrounded, the only resource left was to force their way through numbers unknown to them. The Hessians lost part of their cannon in the town: they did not relish the project of forcing, and were obliged to surrender upon the spot, with all their artillery, six brass pieces, army colors, &c. A Colonel Rawle commanded, who was wounded. The number of prisoners was above 1,200, including officers, — all Hessians. There were few killed or wounded on either side. After having marched off the prisoners and secured the cannon, stores, &c., we returned to the place, nine miles distant, where we had embarked. Providence seemed to have smiled upon every part of this enterprise. Great advantages may be gained from it if we take the proper steps. At another post we have pushed over the river 2,000 men, to-day another body, and to-morrow the whole army will follow. It must give a sensible pleasure to every friend of the rights of man to think with how much intrepidity our people pushed the enemy, and prevented their forming in the town.

" His Excellency the General has done me the unmerited great honor of thanking me in public orders in terms strong and polite. This I should blush to mention to any other than to you, my dear Lucy; and I am fearful that even my Lucy may think her Harry possesses a species of little vanity in doing [it] at all."

" TRENTON, 2d Jan. 1777.

" We are collecting our force at this place, and shall give battle to the enemy very soon. Our people have exerted great fortitude, and stayed beyond the time of their enlistment, in high spirits, but want rum and clothing. Will it give you satisfaction or pleasure in being informed that the Congress have created me a general officer — a brigadier — with the entire command of the artillery?*

* His commission was dated Dec. 27, 1776, the day following the victory of Trenton, but before the news had reached Congress. That body had previously resolved to augment the artillery to a brigade of four regiments.

6

If so, I shall be happy. It was unsolicited on my part, though I cannot say unexpected. People are more lavish in their praises of my poor endeavors than they deserve. All the merit I can claim is industry. I wish to render my devoted country every service in my power; and the only alloy I have in my little exertions is, that it separates me from thee, — the dearest object of all my earthly happiness. May Heaven give us a speedy and happy meeting.

"'The attack of Trenton was a most horrid scene to the poor inhabitants. War, my Lucy, is not a humane trade, and the man who follows [it] as such will meet with his proper demerits in another world."

"MORRISTOWN, Jan. 7, 1777.

"My dearest Love, — I wrote to you from Trenton by a Mr. Furness, which I hope you have received. I then informed you that we soon expected another tussle. I was not out in my conjecture. About three o'clock on the 2d of January, a column of the enemy attacked a party of ours which was stationed about one mile above Trenton. Our party was small, and did not make much resistance. The enemy, who were Hessians, entered the town pell-mell, pretty much in the same manner that we had driven them a few days before.

"Nearly on the other side of Trenton, partly in the town, runs a brook (the Assanpink), which in most places is not fordable, and over which through Trenton is a bridge. The ground on the other side is much higher than on this, and may be said to command Trenton completely. Here it was our army drew up, with thirty or forty pieces of artillery in front. The enemy pushed our small party through the town with vigor, though not with much loss. Their retreat over the bridge was thoroughly secured by the artillery. After they had retired over the bridge, the enemy advanced within reach of our cannon, who saluted them with great vociferation and some execution. This continued till dark, when of course it ceased, except a few shells we now and then chucked into town to prevent their enjoying their new quarters securely. As I before mentioned, the creek was in our front, our left on the Delaware, our right in a wood, parallel to the creek. The situation was strong, to be sure; but hazardous on this account, that had our right wing been defeated, the defeat of the left would almost have been an inevitable consequence, and the whole thrown into confusion or pushed into the Delaware, as it was impassable by boats.

" From these circumstances the general thought it best to attack Princeton, twelve miles in the rear of the enemy's grand army, and where they had the 17th, 40th, and 55th regiments, with a number of draughts, altogether perhaps twelve hundred men. Accordingly, about one o'clock at night we began to march and make this most extra manœuvre. Our troops marched with great silence and order, and arrived near Princeton a little after daybreak. We did not surprise them as at Trenton; for they were on their march down to Trenton, on a road about a quarter of a mile distant from the one in which we were. You may judge of their surprise when they discovered such large columns marching up. They could not possibly suppose it was our army, for that they took for granted was cooped up near Trenton. They could not possibly suppose it was their own army returning by a back road; in short, I believe they were as much astonished as if an army had dropped perpendicularly upon them. However they had not much time for consideration. We pushed a party to attack them. This they repulsed with great spirit, and advanced upon another column just then coming out of a wood, which they likewise put in some disorder; but fresh troops coming up, and the artillery beginning to play, they were after a smart resistance totally put to the rout. The 17th regiment used their bayonets with too much severity upon a party they put to flight; but they were paid for it in proportion, very few escaping. Near sixty were killed on the spot, besides the wounded. We have taken between three and four hundred prisoners, all British troops. They must have lost in this affair nearly five hundred killed, wounded, and prisoners. We lost some gallant officers. Brigadier-General Mercer was wounded: he had three separate stabs with a bayonet. A Lieutenant-Colonel Fleming was killed, and Captain Neil of the artillery, an excellent officer. Mercer will get better.* The enemy took his parole after we left Princeton. We took all their cannon, which consisted of two brass six-pounders, a considerable quantity of military stores, blankets, guns, &c. They lost, among a number of other officers, a Captain Leslie, a son of the Earl of Leven and nephew to General Leslie: him we brought off, and buried with the honors of war.

"After we had been about two hours at Princeton, word was

---

* Mercer's wound proved mortal, and he died on the 12th.

brought that the enemy were advancing from Trenton. This they did, as we have since been informed, in a most infernal sweat, — running, puffing, and blowing, and swearing at being so outwitted. As we had other objects in view, to wit, breaking up their quarters, we pursued our march to Somerset Court House, where there were about thirteen hundred quartered, as we had been informed. They, however, had marched off, and joined the army at Trenton. We at first intended to have made a forced march to Brunswick; but our men having been without either rest, rum, or provisions for two nights and days, were unequal to the task of marching seventeen miles further. If we could have secured one thousand fresh men at Princeton to have pushed for Brunswick, we should have struck one of the most brilliant strokes in all history. However, the advantages are very great : already they have collected their whole force, and drawn themselves to one point, to wit, Brunswick.

"The enemy were within nineteen miles of Philadelphia, they are now sixty miles. We have driven them from almost the whole of West Jersey. The panic is still kept up. We had a battle two days ago with a party of ours and sixty Waldeckers, who were all killed or taken, in Monmouth County in the lower part of the Jerseys. It is not our interest to fight a general battle, nor can I think under all circumstances it is the enemy's. They have sent their baggage to Staten Island from the Jerseys, and we are very well informed they are doing the same from New York. Heath will have orders to march there, and endeavor to storm it on that side. 'There is a tide in the affairs of men, which taken at the flood leads on to victory.' For my part, my Lucy, I look up to heaven and most devoutly thank the great Governor of the Universe for producing this turn in our affairs; and the sentiment I hope will so prevail in the hearts of the people as to induce them to be a people chosen of Heaven, not to give way to despair, but at all times and under all circumstances never to despair of the Commonwealth."

After the battle at Princeton, Knox recommended the march to Morristown, which he had observed to be a good position. The army would be on the enemy's flank, and might easily change its situation if requisite. His earnest importunities prevailed, and winter quarters were there

established. He was then sent on a mission to the eastward, to see to the casting of cannon and the establishment of laboratories, during which he visited his wife at
Boston, whence he writes to the commander-in-chief, under
date of Feb. 1st : —

"After my letter to General Greene from Springfield of the
26th ult., I set out for this place, in order to provide such materials
as were necessary to carry on the various branches connected with
the laboratory and ordnance establishment. Upon my arrival here,
I was much surprised at the very extraordinary bounty offered by
the State ($86⅔) for recruits for the service. Part of a regiment,
consisting of four hundred men with a detachment of one hundred
and fifty artillery, marches to-morrow and next day for Ticonderoga.
The enlistments in this town have been exceeding rapid. General
Ward is here, but whether he acts as a councillor of the Massachusetts or a continental general is difficult to say. There must be one
battalion of artillery raised in this State ; for all the old artillerymen, who have been two years in the service, and acquired some
experience, are from this town and colony. If the Congress should
still adhere to Brookfield in preference to Springfield, it will delay
every thing for three or four months. I wrote General Greene
from Springfield that it was the best place in all the four New England States for a laboratory, cannon foundry, &c., and I hope your
Excellency will order it there."

In the following May we find him associated with Greene
in planning the defences of the North River. On the
eighth, Mrs. Knox writes him from Sewall's Point (Brook-
line, near Boston), where she with her babe had been
undergoing inoculation for the small pox : —
"I have no company here but Madame Heath, who is so
stiff it is impossible to be sociable with her, and Mr.
Gardner the treasurer, so that you may well think what I
feel under my present anxiety." And a few days later
she writes from Boston : —

" A French general (Ducoudray), who styles himself commander-in-chief of the continental artillery, is now in town. He says his appointment is from Mr. Deane, that he is going immediately to head-quarters to take command, that he is a major-general and a deal of it. Who knows but I may have my Harry again? This I am sure of, he will never suffer any one to command him in that department. If he does, he has not the soul which I now think him possessed of."

To his wife, Knox writes from Morristown, on May 20th : —

" From the present information it appears that America will have much more reason to hope for a successful campaign the ensuing summer than she had the last. Our forces come in pretty fast, and are disciplining for the war. We are well supplied with arms and ammunition of all species : this, with the blessing of Heaven, will assist us much ; but, I am sorry to say it, we seem to be *increasing most rapidly in impiety.* This is a bad omen, but I hope we shall mend, though I see no immediate prospect of it. . . . Though your parents are on the opposite side from your Harry, yet it's very strange it should divest them of humanity. Not a line ! My God ! what stuff is the human heart made of ? Although father, mother, sister, and brother have forgotten you, yet, my love, your Harry will ever esteem you the best boon of Heaven."

Again from Camp Middlebrook, 21st June, 1777 : —

" We have the most respectable body of continental troops that America ever had, no going home to-morrow to suck, — hardy, brave fellows, who are as willing to go to heaven by the way of a bayonet or sword as any other mode. With the blessing of Heaven, I have great hopes in the course of this campaign that we shall do something clever. I think in five days there will not be an enemy in the Jerseys ; but I fear they will go up the North River, where perhaps they may plague us more. The inhabitants here appeared as one man, and as people actuated by revenge for the many rapes and murders committed on them. The Congress have taken some precious steps with regard to Mr. Ducoudray. They have resolved that Mr. Deane has exceeded his commission, and that they cannot ratify his treaty with Mr. Ducoudray. Pretty this! — to bring a gentleman 1,200 leagues to affront him."

"CAMP POMPTON PLAINS, 13 July, 1777.

"The letter which I wrote to Congress, to know whether they had appointed Mr. Ducoudray, has, in conjunction with the letter of Generals Sullivan and Greene, produced a resolve purporting 'the said letters to be an infringement on the liberties of the people, as tending to influence the decisions of Congress,' and expecting that we make acknowledgments to them for 'so singular an impropriety.' Conscious of the rectitude of my intention and of the contents of my letter, I shall make no acknowledgments whatever Though my country is too much pressed at present to resign, yet perhaps this campaign will be the last. I am determined to contribute my mite to the defence of the country, in spite of every obstacle."

These officers neither resigned nor made the required apology; and Congress having decided not to ratify Mr. Deane's engagement, the difficulty was removed. Washington had written to the President of Congress and to Mr. R. H. Lee, a member of that body, that the appointment of Ducoudray would cause the retirement of General Knox, "one of the most valuable officers in the service, and who, combating almost innumerable difficulties in the department he fills, has placed the artillery upon a footing that does him the greatest honor;" and he further characterizes him as "a man of great military reading, sound judgment, and clear conceptions."

The opening movements of Sir William Howe's campaign for the acquisition of Philadelphia are thus described in Knox's letter to his intimate friend and life-long correspondent, Harry Jackson, at Boston : —

"CAMP MIDDLEBROOK, 21 June, 1777.

"General Howe on the 14th put his whole army in motion. He had for a long time past been collecting his force from Rhode Island,

New York, Staten Island, &c. The boats upon which he designed
to cross the Delaware as a bridge were fixed on wagons, besides
which he had a large number [of] flat-bottom boats fixed on wagons to transport to the Delaware. These boats with the necessary
apparatus, wagons to convey the baggage and the ammunition
wagons, &c., swelled the number of his wagons to perhaps 1,000
or 1,100, a great incumbrance to an army not very numerous. As
I have before written, our position was exceeding good, and while
we continued on it the passage to the Delaware would be rendered
extremely precarious, and to attack us in camp was an event much
to be wished. However, something was to be done. General Sullivan was posted at Princeton, with a force pretty respectable in
itself, but not sufficient to stop General Howe's army; and he might
by a forced march push a column between Princeton and us, and
cut off General Sullivan's communications at least; but, our intelligence being pretty good, the general directed Sullivan to take
post about four miles from Princeton, in such a manner that the
surrounding him would be impracticable. We also had a party at
Milstone, as a cover for the ammunition to Princeton. This was a
dangerous post from its proximity to the enemy, but rendered less
so by the extreme vigilance which we recommended, and which the
officer commanding particularly obeyed. Matters were thus situated on the morning of the 14th, when we discovered that the
party at Milstone was attacked. Support was immediately sent to
cover the retreat of the party, when it was discovered to be the
enemy's main body, as the same body of observation posted there
were obliged to retreat *pretty quick.*' The enemy took position.
Our whole army was immediately ordered under arms, ready to be
put in motion; but the conduct of the enemy rendered it unnecessary, for instead of immediately pushing for the Delaware, distant
about twenty-five miles, or attacking General Sullivan, he set down
on the ground and instantly began to fortify in a very strong position; but it was not till the next day that we discovered their
works. Their conduct was perplexing. It was unaccountable that
people who the day before gave out in very gasconading terms that
they would be in Philadelphia in six days should stop short when
they had gone only nine miles. The intelligence was pretty good
with respect to their designs, yet it was too imperfect with respect
to their numbers to warrant an attack on troops so well disciplined,

and posted as they were. We also in the course of a day or two discovered that they had not moved with any baggage, even tents and the most necessary, but had come out with an intention of drawing us into the plain ; had left their immense number of wagons behind them, but even in this kind of ostentatious challenge they omitted not one precaution for their own safety. They had Brunswick and the Raritan River on their right, secured by eight or ten strong redoubts. At Brunswick the Raritan bends, and runs a little way north, and then turns nearly west. This they had in their front secured by strong redoubts at Middlebrook. Their left was secured by the river Milstone, which empties itself into the Raritan near Bound Brook : from their right to left was about eight miles.

"In this situation they continued until early in the morning of the 19th, continually at work throwing up redoubts. We had a large body of riflemen, under Colonel Morgan, perpetually making inroads upon them, attacking their pickets, killing their light-horse ; and beset them in such a manner, assisted by the militia, that Mr. Howe, instead of marching to Philadelphia, found himself almost block-aded in an open flat country. Nothing could exceed the spirit shown on this occasion by the much injured people of the Jerseys. Not an atom of the lethargic spirit that possessed them last winter, — all fire, all revenge. The militia of Pennsylvania likewise turned out universally, so that had Sir William put his attempt into exe-cution, we should probably had twenty-five or thirty thousand militia upon his back, besides the most respectable body of conti-nental troops that ever were in America.

"These things being fully represented to General Howe, he thought it proper to take himself and light army back to Brunswick again, and accordingly marched about one o'clock in the morning of the 19th, without beat of drum or sound of fife. When his army had gotten beyond the reach of pursuit, they began to burn, plunder, and waste all before them. The desolation they committed was horrid, and served to show the malice which marks their conduct.

"The militia, light-horse, and riflemen exhibited the greatest marks of valor, frequently taking prisoners within two hundred yards of their encampment. Their loss must be at least one hundred killed and wounded and taken prisoners, among whom are two lieuten-ants of grenadiers of the 55th, and a cornet of light-horse, and a number killed, two sergeants taken. This little march of General

7

Howe's fully proves that no people or country can be permanently conquered where the inhabitants are unanimous in opposition.

"What his next manœuvres may be I can't say, but we suppose the North River; there I believe he will be also disgraced. The motive for belief that the North River will be the scene of his operations is, that intelligence is received that Mr. Burgoyne is about crossing the lakes to Ticonderoga, and General Howe must make an attempt to push for a junction. The enemy from all appearances and advices are upon the eve of evacuating the Jerseys. Times are much altered for them from last fall. The people are unanimous in opposing them: just now four thousand marched off to harass the enemy; as many more will go down towards Brunswick this afternoon."

The subsequent events of the campaign of 1777 in the vicinity of Philadelphia are detailed by Knox in the following letters to his wife and others of his correspondents at Boston: —

TO MRS. KNOX.

"BEVERHOUT, 8 miles north of Morristown,
26th July, 1777.

" General Howe has sailed from the Hook, we suppose for Philadelphia, therefore we are now marching that way. If he is not going [there], then Boston must be his object. We intercepted a letter from him to General Burgoyne, purporting that the expedition up the North River is given up for one to Boston. This letter was designed to fall in our hands, in order to deceive. We suppose he will be at Philadelphia near as soon as we: we are now four days' march from it. Upon the whole, I know he *ought*, in justice to his master, to go either up the North River or the eastward, and endeavor to form a junction with Burgoyne: therefore (if he is not a fool) he will operate accordingly; but we are bound to Philadelphia upon this supposition, and it's very reasonable."

"DERBY, 7 miles below Philadelphia,
25th Aug. 1777.

"The army yesterday marched through the city of Philadelphia. Their excellent appearance and marching astonished the Tories, who are very downcast on the respectability of the army. I was so unhappy as to be absent at this time. General Greene and myself begged the favor of his Excellency's permission to pay a visit to Bethlehem, distant about forty miles, to purchase some things for my dear, dear Lucy. The weather was extremely hot, and we set out at four o'clock in the afternoon, and arrived next morning at nine. An express from the general was waiting for us, with orders to return immediately : he had rode all night. However, we first visited all parts of this singularly happy place, where all the inhabitants seem to vie with each other in humility and brotherly kindness. We joined the army, after a most fatiguing jaunt of a hundred miles yesterday, about an hour after they had passed through Philadelphia."

"WILMINGTON, DEL., 1 Sept. 1777.

" The enemy have landed at the head of Elk, in Maryland, about twenty miles from this. Whether they intend to advance or not is at present uncertain. We shall remain here a few days ; and if they will not come to us, we shall go to them. It is supposed the enemy intend for Philadelphia ; if so, they will meet with a stout opposition. I am at this moment president of a court-martial to try an officer of General Howe for recruiting in the Jerseys."

"CAMP NEAR SCHUYLKILL, 13 Sept. 1777.

" My dear girl will be happy to hear of her Harry's safety; for, my Lucy, Heaven, who is our guide, has protected him in the day of battle. You will hear with this letter of the most severe action that has been fought this war between our army and the enemy. Our people behaved well, but Heaven frowned on us in a degree. We were obliged to retire after very considerable slaughter of the enemy : they dared not pursue a single step. If they advance, we shall fight them again before they get possession of Philadelphia ; but of this they will be cautious. My corps did me great honor : they behaved like men contending for every thing that's valuable." *

* " The regiment of artillery with their general behaved with their usual coolness and intrepidity. Some of them could scarce be prevailed on to quit their guns, even when surrounded by the enemy and forsaken by our infantry. The Boston boys did themselves great honor. I rode up to Captain Allen in the beginning of the action. Young Cooper was with him at the same gun, and a number of our Boston lads : they seemed in high spirits." — *Extract of a Letter from a gentleman of distinction in Philadelphia, Ind. Chronicle,* 2 *Oct.* 1777.

We insert here the account of the battle of Brandy-wine, written by Knox to the President of the Council of Massachusetts : —

"CAMP NEAR SCHUYLKILL, 13th Sept. 1777.

" SIR, — I do myself the honor to transmit to you an account of an action which happened between the American and the British troops, the 11th instant, on the heights of Brandywine.

" Brandywine is a creek which empties itself into the Delaware, near Wilmington, about thirty miles from Philadelphia. On the 9th instant our army took post about eleven miles up this creek, having it in front at a place called Chad's Ford, that being the most probable route by which the enemy would endeavor to pass to Philadelphia. The enemy on the 10th advanced to Kennet Square, within three miles of our advanced parties, and at eight o'clock in the morning of the 11th a considerable body of their army appeared opposite to us. Immediately a heavy cannonade commenced, and lasted with spirit for above two hours, and more or less the whole day. Our advanced light corps, under General Maxwell, engaged the advanced parties of the enemy on the other side of the creek with success, having twice repulsed them, and entirely dispersed a body of 300 Hessians. This light corps was engaged with their advanced parties almost through the day. At the same time this body advanced opposite to our army, another large column, consisting of the British and Hessian grenadiers, light infantry, and some brigades, took a circuitous route of six miles to our right, and crossed the creeks at the forks of Brandywine. His Excellency General Washington, notwith-standing his utmost exertions to obtain intelligence, had very con-tradictory accounts of the numbers and destination of this column until it had crossed the creek six miles to our right. He imme-diately ordered General Sullivan's, Lord Stirling's, and General Stephen's divisions to advance and attack them. This was about three o'clock P.M. These divisions, having advanced about three miles, fell in with the enemy, who were also advancing. Both sides pushed for a hill situated in the middle.

" The contest became exceedingly severe, and lasted without intermission for an hour and a half, when our troops began to give way, having many of them expended all their cartridges.

" His Excellency, who in the beginning of this action galloped to the right, ordered Greene's division and Nash's brigade from the left; but, the distance being so great, the other divisions had retreated before they arrived. However, they formed, and were of the utmost service in covering the retreat of the other divisions, particularly Weedon's brigade of Greene's division, which behaved to admiration in an excessive hot fire, checked the British grenadiers, and finally, after dark, came off in great order.*

"While this scene was acting on the right, the enemy opened a battery on the left of seven pieces of cannon opposite to one of ours of the same number. General Wayne, with a division of the Pennsylvania troops, having Maxwell's light corps on his left, and Nash's brigade (which was afterward drawn off to support the right wing) on his right, formed the left wing. The enemy's batteries and ours kept up an incessant cannonade, and formed such a column of smoke that the British troops passed the creek unperceived on the right of the battery, on the ground which was left unoccupied by the withdrawal of Nash's brigade.

"A very severe action immediately commenced between General Wayne and the enemy, who had now got possession of a height opposite to him. They made several efforts to pass the low grounds between them, and were as frequently repulsed. Night coming on, his Excellency the General gave orders for a retreat, which was regularly effected without the least attempt of the enemy to pursue. Our troops that night retired to Chester, and will now take post in such a manner as best to cover Philadelphia.

"It is difficult at present to ascertain our loss; but, from the most particular inquiry I have been able to make, it will not exceed seven hundred or eight hundred killed, wounded, and missing, and ten field-pieces.

* In a letter to Rev. Dr. Gordon, then about leaving for England, where his History of the American Revolution was to be published, Knox, under date of New York, 11th March, 1786, gives the composition of Weedon's brigade, which behaved with conspicuous gallantry at Brandywine. In it were Colonel Walter Stewart's Pennsylvania regiment, and the Virginia regiments of Colonel Spotswood (3d), Lieutenant-Colonel Hendricks (6th), Colonel Ed. Stevens (10th), and (14th) Colonel Lewis, who was afterward wounded at Guilford, where he commanded a brigade of militia. Knox furnished the Doctor with other materials for his work, and closes his letter thus: "I observe," he says, "the printers are exceedingly angry with you at Boston for the intention of printing it [Gordon's History] in Great Britain, and some of the squibs are republished here."

" It is a common practice in war to diminish our own loss and magnify that of our enemy; but, from my own observation and the opinion of others, their loss must be much greater than ours."

POTTSGROVE, 24 Sept. 1777.

" I wrote you on the 13th. The same day we crossed the Schuylkill, in order to try the issue of another appeal to *Him who directs all human events*. After some days' manœuvring, we came in sight of the enemy, and drew up in order of battle, which the enemy declined; but a most violent rain coming on obliged us to change our position, in the course of which nearly all the musket cartridges of the army that had been delivered to the men were damaged, consisting of above 400,000. This was a most terrible stroke to us, and owing entirely to the badness of the cartouch-boxes which had been provided for the army.

" This unfortunate event obliged us to retire, in order to get supplied with so essential an article as cartridges, after which we forded the Schuylkill, in order to be opposite to the enemy; accordingly we took post at a place called Flatland Ford.

" A defensive war is the most difficult to guard against, because one is always obliged to attend to the feints of the enemy. To defend an extensive river when it is unfordable is almost impossible; but when fordable in every part, it becomes impracticable. On the afternoon of the 21st the enemy made a most rapid march of ten or twelve miles to our right: this obliged us to follow them. They kindled large fires, and in the next night marched as rapidly back and crossed at a place where we had few guards, and pushed towards Philadelphia, and will this morning enter the city without opposition. We fought one battle for it, and it was no deficiency in bravery that lost us the day. Philadelphia, it seems, has been their favorite object. Their shipping has not joined them there. They will first have to raise the *chevaux de frise* in the Delaware, and defeat the naval force there, which is considerable.

" The troops in this excursion of ten days without baggage suffered excessive hardships, — without tents in the rain, several marches of all night, and often without sufficient provision. This they endured with the perseverance and patience of good soldiers. Generals Smallwood, Wayne, McDougall, and a considerable body of militia, will join us to-day and to-morrow. This day we shall move towards Philadelphia, in order to try the fortune of another battle, in which we devoutly hope the blessing of Heaven. I consider the loss of Philadelphia as only temporary, — to be recovered when expedient. It is no more than the loss of Boston, nor, in my opinion, half so much, when the present trade of the latter be considered. It is situated on a point of land formed by the rivers Delaware and Schuylkill, so that it would [have] been highly improper to have thrown ourselves into it.

"If the enemy do not get their shipping up soon, and go into Philadelphia, they will be in a very ineligible situation. I do not in the present circumstances consider Philadelphia of so much consequence as the loss of reputation to our arms; but I trust in God we shall soon make up that matter. Billy* is well, and undergoes the hardships of the campaign surprisingly well, and they are neither few nor small."

TO COLONEL HENRY JACKSON.†

"CAMP AT METUCHIN, 20 miles from Philadelphia,
3d Oct. '77.

"MY DEAR HARRY, — The enemy are now encamped at Philadelphia and its environs for about six miles. The Delaware frigate was given up to them in a manner scandalous to relate. The crew, it's said, after they had fired one broadside at a battery which was erecting near the city, ran her ashore, and gave her up to the Britons. The crew were principally foreigners. Our army has had several reinforcements of militia, &c., since the late action. I hope for better success in the next; and an action we shall most assuredly have before they or we go into winter quarters."

* His brother William had joined him in July, as his secretary, and behaved with spirit a few days later at Germantown.

† Jackson had been appointed colonel of one of the additional continental battalions to be raised in Massachusetts, and numbered the 16th. He was born in Boston in 1748, and died there 4 Jan. 1809 ; commissioned colonel 12 Jan. 1777; distinguished at Monmouth, in Sullivan's Rhode Island campaign, and at Springfield, N.J.; and commanded the last body of continental soldiers disbanded in 1784 ; major-general first division Massachusetts militia, 1792–96; and, as United States agent, superintended the construction of the frigate "Constitution." Jackson was the intimate friend and correspondent of Knox, for whom he acted as a business agent in many important transactions. Many of his letters, which are exceedingly interesting, are preserved in the Knox Papers.

Washington having been reinforced by troops from Peekskill on the Hudson, and knowing that Howe had weakened his army by detachments for the reduction of the posts on the Delaware, resolved to attack his main division at Germantown.

The following account of the battle of Germantown was written by Knox to Hon. Artemas Ward, President of the Council of Massachusetts Bay.

"ARTILLERY PARK, PERKEOMY CREEK, Oct. 7, 1777
(27 miles from Philadelphia).

"SIR, — I shall endeavor to give you a short authentic account of an attack made by our army on the British army, lying at Germantown, six miles from Philadelphia, on the morning of the 4th instant.

"At six o'clock on the evening of the 3d, the army, under his Excellency General Washington, began their march in four columns on as many roads towards the enemy; the nearest column had to march fourteen, and some twenty, miles. By marching all night, the columns arrived a little after break of day [opposite] to the respective posts of the enemy assigned to them. The attack commenced by forcing their pickets, which were soon reinforced in front by all the light infantry of the line and other troops. After a smart action, these were obliged to give way, our troops pressing on with great spirit and good order.

"The different attacks being made at the same time distracted the enemy's attention so much, that after about an hour's engagement they began to give way on every part; but, most unfortunately for us, a fog which had arisen about daybreak became so excessively thick from the continued firing that it was impossible to discover an object at twenty yards' distance.

"This was the unhappy cause of our losing the victory after being in possession of it for near two hours, and having driven the enemy above two miles from the place where the engagement begun, quite through their encampment. In this unusual fog it was impossible to know how to support, or what part to push. At this instant, the enemy again rallied and obliged part of our troops to retire; and after a smart resistance, the retreat of the line became general. The enemy followed with caution, and we came off without the loss of a single piece of cannon or any thing else, except one empty ammunition wagon, the engagement from beginning to end being about two hours and forty minutes.

"Our loss in killed, wounded, and missing, is not fully ascertained, but will not exceed five hundred or six hundred. We had a very considerable number of officers of merit killed and wounded. Brigadier-General Nash, of North Carolina, mortally wounded by a cannon-ball taking off his thigh.

"The enemy's loss, we hear from pretty good authority, is very considerable. General Agnew killed. Sir William Erskine wounded. This is the first attack made during this war by the American troops on the main body of the enemy; and had it not been [for] the unlucky circumstance of the fog, Philadelphia would probably have been in our hands. It is matter worthy of observation that in most other countries which have been invaded one or two battles have decided their fate; but America rises after a defeat!

"We were more numerous after the battle of Brandywine than before, and we have demonstration of being more numerous now than before the 4th. Our men are in the highest spirits, and ardently desire another trial. I know of no ill consequences that can follow the late action; on the contrary, we have gained considerable experience, and our army have a certain proof that the British troops are vulnerable."

In a letter to Mrs. Knox he says: "To this cause [the fog], in conjunction with the enemy's taking possession of some stone buildings in Germantown, is to be ascribed the loss of the victory. We brought off the greater part of our wounded."

TO MRS. KNOX.

"CAMP, 24 miles from Philadelphia, 13th Oct. 1777.

. . . "I send you this by Captain Randall, who has the misfortune to be again made a prisoner, after being slightly wounded in seven or eight places.

"The matter you mention about rations cannot be complied with,

8

and I thank God I have too much reliance on his divine providence
to have any of those misgivings and forebodings of which my dear
Lucy seems so apprehensive. I trust the same Divine Being who
brought us together will support us. The enemy have not yet reduced our obstacles in the river Delaware below Philadelphia, and
consequently have not got their shipping up to the town. They have
made several efforts, but hitherto in vain, in one of which we took
two officers and fifty-six privates prisoners. If the enemy cannot
get their shipping up, Philadelphia is one of the most ineligible
places in the world for an army surrounded by rivers which are
impassable, and an army above them. We have been pretty quiet
since the action of the 4th; but we have yet tolerable prospects
and hopes to winter in Philadelphia. I mean our army; for however clouded the prospect may be, yet I have sanguine hopes of
being able to live this winter in sweet fellowship with the dearest
friend of my heart. Ere you receive this, you will receive the
account of the loss of Fort Montgomery, which I own to you is in
my opinion exceedingly heavy, but it must stimulate us to make
greater exertions. America almost deserves to be made slaves for
her non-exertions in so important an affair. . . . Observe, my dear
girl, how Providence supports us. The advantages gained by our
Northern army give almost a decisive turn to the contest. For my
own part I have not yet seen so bright a dawn as the prospect, and
I am as perfectly convinced in my own mind of the kindness of
Providence towards us as I am of my own existence."

TO THE SAME.

"CAMP, 10 miles from Philadelphia, Nov. 8, 1777.

. . . . "The enemy have not yet been able to drive our galleys
away, or storm or batter our forts with success. We have lately
had a storm, which has ruined their batteries and works erected
against Fort Mifflin. Since they had two men-of-war burnt on the
23d in the river, and were defeated the 22d at Red Bank, they
have appeared quite silent in deeds, but not so in words. They have
been very angry for our *feux de joie*, which we have fired on the
several victories over Burgoyne, and say that by and by [we] shall
bring ourselves into contempt with our own army for propagating
such known falsehoods. Poor fellows! nothing but Britain must
triumph."

On the 15th of November, after the fall of Fort Mifflin, Knox, with De Kalb and St. Clair, was sent to provide for the security of Red Bank. This post, known as Fort Mercer, fell, however, after a brave defence on the 18th.

In the council of war on Oct. 26, and again on Dec. 3d, Knox opposed the project of an attack on the enemy's lines at Philadelphia, giving on the day last named these reasons : " Our entire want of clothing ; the impossibility and impracticability of surprising 10,000 veteran troops in a well fortified city ; the impossibility of our keeping the field to besiege their works and city regularly, being almost totally deficient in warlike apparatus for so arduous an enterprise ; and the uncertainty of obtaining a sufficient number of militia to warrant the enterprise." He proposed that the army go into winter quarters, with the right at Lancaster and the left at Reading, provided a sufficiency of houses and good cover could be had there ; if not, that it should be hutted about thirty miles from Philadelphia, near the Schuylkill. The army wintered at Valley Forge, somewhat nearer the city ; and Knox took advantage of the cessation of active operations to visit his wife at Boston. A picture of the privations of the army during this memorable winter is given in the following letter from Greene to Knox : —

"CAMP, VALLEY FORGE, 26th Feb. 1778.

"The army has been in great distress since you left it. The troops are getting naked ; they were seven days without meat, and several days without bread. Such patience and moderation as they manifested under their sufferings does the highest honor to the magnanimity of the American soldiers. The seventh day they came before their superior officers, and told their sufferings in as respectful terms as if they had been humble petitioners for special favors. They added that it would be impossible to continue in camp any longer without support. Happily relief arrived from the little collections I and some others had made, and prevented the army from disbanding. We are still in danger of starving. Hundreds of our horses have already starved to death. The committee of Congress have seen all these things with their own eyes. They have been urging me for several days to accept the quartermaster-general's appointment, his Excellency also presses it upon me exceedingly. I hate the place, but hardly know what to do. I wish for your advice in the affair, but am obliged to determine immediately."

Mrs. Knox arrived in camp at Valley Forge on May 20, 1778, soon after the news of the alliance with France had been received. She was attended from New Haven by General Arnold, who was of great service to her during her journey, and remained with the army until it was disbanded.

At the battle of Monmouth, which occurred on June 28th, and of which he ever after spoke with much pride, Knox reconnoitred in front, rallying the retreat, and bringing up the rear with a brisk fire from a battery planted in the night, directed by his brigade adjutant, the chevalier Mauduit Duplessis. Of the services of this arm, Washington, in general orders, says he " can with pleasure inform General Knox and the officers of the artillery that the enemy has done them the justice to acknowledge that no artillery could have been better served than ours."

To his brother and to his wife, Knox wrote the particulars of this battle, and of the events which preceded it : —

TO HIS BROTHER WILLIAM.

HOPEWELL TOWNSHIP, NEW JERSEY,
4 o'clock A.M., 25th June, 1778.

" The enemy evacuated Philadelphia on the 19th. Lucy and I went in, but it stunk so abominably that it was impossible to stay there, as was her first design. The enemy are now at Allen Town, about ten miles southeast of Princeton, and we are at about six

miles north [of] Princeton, so that the two armies are now
about nineteen or twenty miles apart. We are now on the march
towards them, and their movements this day will determine whether
we shall come in close contact with each other. We have now very
numerous parties harassing and teasing them on all quarters.
Desertion prevails exceedingly in their army, especially among the
Germans. Above three hundred German and English have de-
serted since they left Philadelphia. Had we a sufficiency of numbers, we should be able to force them to a similar treaty with
Burgoyne ; but, at present, have not quite such sanguine hopes.
If general actions had no other consequences than merely the killed
and wounded, we should attack them in twenty-four hours. But
the fate of posterity, and not the illusive brilliancy of military glory,
governs our Fabian commander, the man [to whom], under God,
America owes her present prospects of peace and happiness."

TO MRS. KNOX.

"June 29, near Monmouth Court House.

"MY DEAREST LOVE, — I wrote you some few days ago that a
day or two would determine whether we should have an engagement with the Britons. Yesterday, at about nine o'clock A.M., our
advanced parties under General Lee attacked their rear while on
the march towards Shrewsbury, upon which their whole army,
except the Hessians, came to the right about; and, after some fighting, obliged him to retire to the main army, which was about two
miles distant. The enemy advanced with great spirit to the attack,
and began a very brisk cannonade on us, who were formed to
receive them.

"The cannonade lasted from about eleven until six o'clock, at
which time the enemy began to retire on all quarters, and left us
in possession of the field. We have had several field officers killed,
and a considerable number of others. Colonel Ramsay, Mrs. Ramsay's husband, was taken prisoner, and this morning released on
his parole. I have had several officers killed and wounded. My
brave lads behaved with their usual intrepidity, and the army gave
the corps of artillery their full proportion of the glory of the day.

"Indeed, upon the whole, it is very splendid. The capital army
of Britain defeated and obliged to retreat before the Americans,

whom they despised so much! I cannot ascertain either our or the enemy's loss, but I really think they have lost three times the number we have. I judge from the field of battle, which, to be sure, is a field of carnage and blood: three to one of the British forces lie there. The Britons confess they have never received so severe a check. The enemy took a strong post, about a mile from the place of action, to dislodge them from which, as it was dark, would cost too many men, and by which they covered the retreat of their army. After having been fighting all day, and one of the hottest I ever felt, they decamped in the night and marched off with the utmost precipitation, leaving a great number of their wounded, both officers and men, in our hands. We have sent out large bodies in pursuit, but I believe they will not be able to come up with the main body. . . . The number of deserters, since they left Philadelphia, must exceed eight hundred. The march has proved to them a most destructive one, and is very ill-calculated to give Sir H. Clinton any *éclat*. He may storm Fort Montgomery, but is very ill-calculated, in my opinion, to be at the head of a large army.

"My friend, Harry [Jackson], crossed over from Philadelphia, and was in the unfortunate [*i.e.*, early] part of the day. I saw him once on the field, for a moment: he appeared much fatigued. His regiment had a few killed and wounded, and is reported to have behaved well."   •

TO HIS BROTHER WILLIAM.

"CAMP BRUNSWICK, 3d July, 1778.

. . . "The enemy inclined more to their right than we expected, and took the road to Sandy Hook, instead of the supposed one to South Amboy.

"A body of Jersey militia, amounting to near 2,000, had endeavored to retard them, by taking up the bridges, felling trees, and harassing their flanks and rear. Beside these, his Excellency General Washington had detached several large bodies for the same purpose, all of which, except Colonel Morgan, were, on the 28th ult., united under General Lee, who early on that morning advanced to Monmouth Court House with the intention of attacking the covering party by left flank, the main army moving on at the same time to support him, although it was some miles in the rear. The parties under General Lee, instead of finding a covering party as was expected, found their whole army or the greater part of it. After some manœuvring, cannonading, and some other circumstances, which are not yet sufficiently explained, it was thought proper by General Lee to retire until it met the main army, which it effected without much loss. The army was drawn up on advantageous ground to receive the enemy, who advanced to the attack with considerable impetuosity, and began a brisk cannonade, which was returned with becoming spirit. The action of the musketry was various, and with intermissions until about six o'clock, when we pushed the enemy off the field. . . . Their whole loss may amount to about ten or twelve hundred killed, wounded, and prisoners. His Excellency, the General, has done the corps of artillery and me the honor to notice us in general orders in very pointed and flattering terms. Indeed, I was highly delighted with their coolness, bravery, and good conduct. The effects of the *Battle of Monmouth* will be great and lasting. It will convince the enemy and the world that nothing but a good constitution is wanting to render our army equal to any in the world."

From letters to his brother at various times we extract as follows: —

"CAMP, WHITE PLAINS, 14th Sept. 1778.

. . . "We wish to know where Lord Howe is, as it might be some clew to the designs of the enemy; though as to dangerous designs, they have none, I am persuaded, nor never had, except to themselves. It is improper for a person in my station to speak thus, were it to be divulged; but I do not believe there ever was a set of men so perfectly disqualified, by a total and profound ignorance of every thing that ought to constitute the characters of leaders of an army to conquest. I beg you not to imagine that by depreciation of their abilities I mean to exalt our own. God forbid! I shall say nothing about it but only this, that we never set ourselves up as great military men. I believe they [the enemy] are about to *quit* the continent, and perhaps *only* wait for their last orders to effect it."

"PHILADELPHIA, 3 Feb. 1779.

. . . "We are in great want of lead. The Board of War have desired me to write to Boston to inquire what quantity can be gotten there and at the neighboring towns, and at what price. I wish you to make the inquiry, or rather to get some person to make it for you, as the gentlemen speculators may suspect from your connection that you want it for the public, and advance their prices in proportion. Write me the result speedily as possible, so that I may communicate it to the board. . . . I am glad you have gotten into the old store. I thank you for the little pamphlet. The girls are the same everywhere, — at least some of them: they love a red coat dearly. Arnold is going to be married to a beautiful and accomplished young lady, — a Miss Shippen, of one of the best families in this place."

"Feb. 13.

. . . "You will see in the papers some highly colored charges against General Arnold, by the State of Pennsylvania. I shall be exceedingly mistaken if one of them can be proven.' He has returned to Philadelphia, and will, I hope, be able to vindicate himself from the aspersions of his enemies."

"PLUCKEMIN, 28 Feb. 1779.

. . . "You wish to know my business to Philadelphia. It was merely to get the ordnance department better regulated. Besides the satisfaction of having the business of the public done better, the only advantage that will result to me will be some pay expressly for the management of the ordnance department in the field. I undoubtedly might have at first stipulated for some pecuniary advantages for myself; but I know not how it is, I do not approve of money obtained in the public service: it does not appear to me, in a war like ours, to be right, and I cannot bring myself to think differently, although poverty may be the consequence. We had at the Park [of artillery], on the 18th, a most genteel entertainment given by self and officers. Everybody allowed it to be the first of the kind ever exhibited in this State at least. We had about seventy ladies, all of the first *ton* in the State, and between three and four hundred gentlemen. We danced all night, — an elegant room. The illuminating, fireworks, &c., were more than pretty. It was to celebrate the alliance between France and America."

"March 13.

"I am sorry for the loss of the vessel you mention, but not discouraged. I hope the little vessel will at least make up for her. I wrote to you to try something, by way of adventure, in the 'General Arnold.' She is a good vessel and commander. . . . I am exceedingly anxious to effect something in these fluctuating times, which may make us lazy for life. You know my sentiments with respect to making any thing out of the public. I abominate the idea. I could not, at the end of the war, mix with my fellow-citizens with that conscious integrity, the felicity of which I often anticipate."

Knox seems to have been unfortunate in his privateering speculations, vessel after vessel in which he had a share being captured by the enemy, some of them with valuable cargoes and just as they were entering port.

"PLUCKEMIN, N.J., 7 May, 1779.

"If we are to believe Rivington's paper of May 1, we are to have bloody work this summer. They swear by monstrous big oaths they will exterminate us this campaign. However that *may* be, we at present have but little apprehensions of it, although, from a variety of corroborating circumstances, we expect we shall have a much more active campaign than the last."

In a later letter he says : —

"The whole army have moved up to this place [Middlebrook] to cover the almost infinitely important posts in the highlands, which we do in so effectual a manner that, were the enemy much stronger than they are, I should be in no pain for the safety of the posts. The enemy have established themselves so securely at King's Ferry that we shall not be able to dislodge them at present. Perhaps a future and more important operation may involve the posts at King's Ferry in its fall. The enemy expect reinforcements, and we, with the blessing of Heaven, expect to baffle their utmost efforts. We expect every thing from the discipline and goodness of our troops; but probably we shall want some assistance from our brethren."

9

Of the warmth of Knox's affection for his friend General Lincoln, his letters give ample evidence. Here is an extract from one written just after the capture of Charleston by Sir Henry Clinton, where Lincoln and his army became prisoners.

" The great defence made by you and your garrison in field fortifications will confer on you and them the esteem and admiration of every sensible military man. I hope and believe that Congress will most unequivocally bestow that applause which you have so richly merited. No event, except the capture of Sir II. Clinton and his army, would give me more pleasure than to see you. IIe is now in force at Springfield, below Morristown."

And at a later period he writes : —

" The first moment I had the happiness of being acquainted with you I conceived a high degree of friendship, which uniformly has increased as I became more intimate, until the present period. I consider the confidential manner in which we have indulged as one of the happy circumstances of my life, and in all events of grief or joy there is no man from whose friendship I should more readily expect the most cordial balsam, or whose bosom would more cheerfully expand in a participation of my happiness."

The French army under the Count de Rochambeau, destined to co-operate with the Americans, arrived at Newport in July, 1780; and on Sept. 21st, Knox, with Washington and La Fayette, visited the French general and admiral, de Ternay, at Hartford, to concert the details of a plan of operations. While returning from this meeting, they heard of Arnold's treason, and immediately hastened to West Point.

Knox was one of the board of general officers which tried and condemned Major André to death as a spy, a sentence which the usages of war compelled them to pronounce, but which was especially distasteful to him since

62

:::::::::::::::::::::::::::::::::

63.

that chance meeting on Lake George, narrated on a previous page, when they had made each other's acquaintance under such peculiar circumstances.

In the latter part of November, the Chevalier de Chastellux, a major-general in Rochambeau's army and a member of the French Academy, visited the American camp at New Windsor. From his Travels, published a few years later, we extract the following interesting particulars of this visit.

In the morning while at breakfast, horses were brought and orders given for the men to get under arms, and the chevalier and Washington repaired to the camp, where they were received by General Knox at the head of his artillery. This was exhibited in fine order, formed in the foreign manner, each gunner at his post ready to fire. Knox politely apologized for not firing a salute, on account of the troops on the other side of the river, which had been put in motion by a previous order, and whom he was afraid of giving some alarm.

Returning from a subsequent tour to visit the general officers of the line at their respective quarters with La Fayette, they met with Knox, who brought them back to head-quarters by the nearest way through a wood, where they fell into a road leading to his retired residence. This was a little rural spot where Mrs. Knox had passed part of the campaign; and here the chevalier found what he called a *real* " family," formed besides the general and his wife of a little girl of three years and an infant of six months.

The wretched situation of the army at this time, which culminated in the mutiny of the lines of Pennsylvania and New Jersey, is graphically described in this extract from Knox's letter to his brother, dated Dec. 2, 1780 : —

" We depend upon the great Author of Nature to provide subsistence and clothing for us through a long and severe winter; for the people, whose business, according to the common course of things, it was to provide the materials necessary, have either been unable or neglected to do it. The soldier, ragged almost to nakedness, has to sit down at this period, and with an axe — perhaps his only tool, and probably that a bad one — to make his habitation for winter. However, this, and [being] punished with hunger into the bargain, the soldiers and officers have borne with a fortitude almost superhuman. The country must be grateful to these brave fellows. It is impossible to admit of the idea of an alternative."

In January, 1781, he was sent by Washington to the Eastern States to represent the suffering condition of the troops with a view to their relief, and on the 14th arrived at Boston with the news of the mutiny of the Pennsylvania line.

An active campaign was now planned which, with the aid of our allies, it was hoped would be decisive. Washington, on Feb. 16, wrote to Knox, instructing him to procure the articles necessary to a "capital operation against New York, or against Charleston, Savannah, Penobscot, &c., in case of inability to undertake the siege of the first and principal object." Knox in reply promised his utmost efforts to obtain the requisite supplies, but details the great want of proper *material* for such an operation, and complains of the Board of War for neglecting his repeated requisitions. "Powder," he says, " is an article of which we are so deficient that, when a reasonable quantity shall be appropriated for the use of the important posts in the highlands (which ought and will be furnished under all circumstances), there will literally none remain."

The following letters and extracts of letters throw light upon the occurrences of this eventful campaign.

" WETHERSFIELD, 20 May, 1781.

"I am here, my dear brother, having arrived last evening with his Excellency the General and General Duportail to meet Count Rochambeau and Admiral Barras, upon some matters of great consequence. We came here last night. The French gentlemen will be here to-morrow, and we shall probably depart in two days after."

And on the 25th he writes him : —

" We have not finished our business until this morning. Count Rochambeau left us yesterday, and we shall set out in about one hour, and shall expect to reach New Windsor to-morrow evening."

At this important meeting the plan of the subsequent campaign was discussed, and as far as possible decided on, the primary object being New York.

WASHINGTON TO KNOX.

" HEAD-QUARTERS, NEW WINDSOR, May 28, 1781.

" As you are perfectly acquainted with the measures which have been concerted with the Count de Rochambeau, I have only to request that you will be pleased to make all the necessary estimates of articles wanted in your department, and also put the whole business for the operation (so far as is within your reach) in the best train of execution which our embarrassed circumstances will possibly admit. Under the present appearances of an evacuation of New York, I think it will be [proper] to draw the stores from the eastward rather than from the southward."

TO WILLIAM KNOX.

" CAMP AT PHILLIPSBURG, 10 miles from King's Bridge,
20 July, 1781.

" Lucy, with her sweet children, has gone up the river with Mrs. Cochran, on a visit to some families. I suppose she will proceed as far as Albany; after which, I think, she will sit down in Jersey for the remainder of the campaign. Although we are not bad in ac-

"I am sending aide-de-camp after aide-de-camp to get news from the northward. I am not a little apprehensive the people on the road will think the Southern army is broken up.

"I beg you will present Mrs. Knox with my most affectionate regards; and I hope you will not get in the way of a four-and-twenty pounder, but will return to her with whole bones. My compliments to honest Shaw."

And again : —

"Sept. 29, 1781.

"My DEAR FRIEND, — Where you are I know not, but if you are where I wish you, it is with the General in Virginia; the prospect is so bright and the glory so great, that I want you to be there to share in them. I was in hopes you would have operated seriously against New York, which would have been still more important; but as your operations are directed another way, I take it for granted means were wanting to play the great game.

" We have been beating the bush, and the General has come to catch the bird. Never was there a more inviting object to glory. The General is a most fortunate man, and may success and laurels attend him. We have fought frequently and bled freely, and little glory comes to our share. Our force has been so small that nothing capital could be effected, and our operations have been conducted under every disadvantage that could embarrass either a general or an army.

"I long to see you, and spend an evening's conversation together. Where is Mrs. Knox? and how is Lucy and my young god-son, Sir Harry? I beg you will present my kind compliments and best wishes to Mrs. Knox.

" How is my old friend, Colonel Jackson? — is he as fat as ever, and can he still eat down a plate of fish that he can't see over? God bless his fat soul with good health and good spirits to the end of the war, that we may all have a happy meeting in the North. Please to give my compliments to your brother, and tell him we are catching at smoky glory while he is wisely treasuring up solid coin."

On the 19th of August, Washington, learning of the expected arrival of the fleet of De Grasse, marched his

army to the southward, having abandoned the attempt upon New York, in order to operate, in conjunction with the French military and naval forces, against Lord Cornwallis in Virginia. He reached Williamsburg on September 14, and, accompanied by Rochambeau, Chastellux, Knox, and Duportail, immediately repaired to the fleet of De Grasse, and a plan of co-operation was arranged on board the " Ville de Paris." Expecting an attack from a British fleet not much inferior to his own, and thinking his station within the Chesapeake unfavorable for a naval combat, the French admiral a few days later designed to put to sea with his fleet in quest of the British. This alarmed the American commander, who despatched La Fayette and Knox to entreat him to preserve his station, in which they fortunately prevailed.

The following letters, relating to the investiture and siege of Yorktown, are not uninteresting, that to Mr. Jay, our minister to Spain, giving a full account of the Virginia campaign : —

TO WILLIAM KNOX.

"HEAD OF ELK, 8 Sept. 1781.

" I rob my business of one moment to inform you that our army is here, and will, with all its stores, proceed down the Chesapeake in three days. Our prospects are good ; and I shall hope to inform you, in fifteen days, that we have had Cornwallis completely invested. The Count de Grasse's squadron is a noble one, and will prevent the enemy's escape by water. I hope we shall do it by land.

" Lucy leaves her daughter in Philadelphia, and in five or six days will set out for Virginia to reside with Mrs. Washington."

TO MRS. KNOX AT MOUNT VERNON.

"CAMP BEFORE YORK, 1 Oct. 1781.

" We came before York on the 28th, on the 29th nearly completed the investiture ; but yesterday the enemy evacuated their

10

outposts, which gives us a considerable advantage in point of time. Our prospects are good, and we shall soon hope to impress our haughty foe with a respect for the continental arms."

TO MRS. KNOX.

"CAMP BEFORE YORK, eight o'clock A.M., 19 Oct. 1781.

" I have detained William until this moment that I might be the first to communicate *good news* to the charmer of my soul. A glorious moment for America! This day Lord Cornwallis and his army march out and pile their arms in the face of our victorious army. The day before yesterday he desired commissioners might be named to treat of the surrender of his troops, the ships, and every thing they possess. He at first requested that the Britons might be sent to Britain, and the Germans to Germany; but this the General refused, and they have now agreed to surrender prisoners of war, to be kept in America until exchanged or released. They will have the same *honors* as the garrison of Charleston ; that is, they *will not* be permitted to unfurl their colors, or *play Yankee Doodle*. We know not yet how many they are. The General has just requested me to be at head-quarters instantly, therefore I cannot be more particular."

TO JOHN JAY.

"CAMP BEFORE YORK, IN VIRGINIA, 21 Oct. 1781.

" The enemy's operations in these States, though not carried on with great armies, compared with those of 1776 and 1777, yet were so formidable as to dispel every force which the country of itself was capable of opposing. This rendered it necessary for America to march its army here, or give up the Southern States as lost. It appears, also, to have been the opinion of the French Court, as Count de Grasse gave intelligence of his intention of arriving at the Capes of Virginia. Our previous views were New York. The dispositions were made on the Hudson's River for the attack of Lord Cornwallis in Virginia, and every thing has succeeded equal to our sanguine wishes.

" This important affair has been effected by the most harmonious concurrence of circumstances that could possibly have happened : a fleet and troops from the West Indies, under the orders of one of the best men in the world; an army of American and French troops, marching from the North River,—five hundred miles,—and the fleet of Count de Barras, all joining so exactly in point of time as to render what has happened almost certain.

"I shall not enter into a detail of circumstances previous to the collection of our force at Williamsburg, twelve miles distant from this place, which was made on the 27th ult. On the 28th we marched to the camp, and on the 29th and 30th we completed the investiture of York. A body of American militia, Lauzun's legion, and some marines from the fleet of Count de Grasse, at the same time formed in the vicinity of Gloucester, so as to prevent any incursions of the enemy into the country. From the 1st October to the 6th was spent in preparing our materials for the siege, bringing forward our cannon and stores, and in reconnoitring the points of attack. On the evening of the 6th we broke ground and began our first parallel within six hundred yards of the enemy's works, undiscovered.

"The first parallel, four redoubts, and all our batteries were finished by the 9th, at two o'clock P.M., when we opened our batteries and kept them playing continually. On the night of the 12th we began our second parallel, at three hundred yards' distance from the enemy. And on the night of the 14th we stormed the two redoubts which the enemy had in advance of their main works. The gallant troops of France under the orders of Baron de Viomenil, and the hardy soldiers of America under the Marquis de la Fayette, attacked separate works and carried them in an instant. This brilliant stroke was effected without any great loss on our side: the enemy lost between one and two hundred. This advantage was important, and gave us an opportunity of perfecting our second parallel, into which we took the two redoubts. On the 16th, just before day, the enemy made a sortie, and spiked up some of our cannon, but were soon repulsed and driven back to their works. The cannon were soon cleared; and the same day our batteries in the second parallel began the fire, and continued without intermission until nine o'clock in the morning of the 17th October, ever memorable on account of the Saratoga affair, when the enemy sent a flag, offering to treat of the surrender of the posts of York and Gloucester. The firing continued until two o'clock, when commissioners on both sides met to adjust the capitulation, which was not finished and signed until twelve o'clock on the 19th. Our troops took possession of two redoubts of the enemy soon after, and about two o'clock the enemy marched out and grounded their arms.

" 'The whole garrison are prisoners of war, and had the same honors only as were granted to our garrison at Charleston, — *their colors were cased*, and they were prohibited playing a French or American tune.

" The returns are not yet collected ; but including officers, sick, and well, there are more than seven thousand, exclusive of seamen, who are supposed to amount to one thousand. There are near forty sail of topsail vessels in the harbor, about one-half of which the enemy sunk upon different occasions ; about two hundred pieces of cannon, nearly one-half of them brass ; a great number of arms, drums, and colors are among the trophies of this decisive stroke. The prisoners are to be sent into any part of this State, Maryland, or Pennsylvania. The consequences will be extensively beneficial. The enemy will immediately be confined to Charleston and New York, and reduced to a defensive war of those two posts, for which they have not more troops in America than to form adequate garrisons."

Knox's skill and activity in providing and forwarding heavy cannon for the siege of Yorktown caused Washington to report to the President of Congress that " the resources of his genius supplied the deficit of means ; " and he was complimented in general orders after the surrender, and recommended for promotion. Chastellux, in his " Travels in North America," also pays him a high compliment. " We cannot," he says, " sufficiently admire the intelligence and activity with which he collected from different places and transported to the batteries more than thirty pieces of cannon and mortars of large calibre, for the siege." Again he says : " The artillery was always very well served, the general incessantly directing it and often himself pointing the mortars : seldom did he leave the batteries. . . . The English marvelled at the exact fire and the terrible execution of the French artillery ; and we marvelled no less at the extraordinary progress of the

American artillery, and at the capacity and instruction of
the officers. As to General Knox, but one-half has been
said in commending his military genius. He is a man of
talent, well instructed, of a buoyant disposition, ingenuous
and true : it is impossible to know him without esteeming
and loving him." In a letter to Knox, of March 30, 1782,
he thus manifests the warmth of his friendship : —

"My sentiments will always meet yours, and I hope that I shall
not be excelled in serving America and loving General Knox.
Let us be brothers in arms, and friends in time of peace. Let the
alliance between our respective countries dwell in our bosoms, where
it shall find a perfect emblem of the two powers : in mine, the
seniority ; in yours, the extent of territory.

"I depend upon your faith, and pledge my honor that no interest
in the world can prevail over the warm and firm attachment with
which I have the honor to be   DE CHASTELLUX."

General Greene thus congratulates his friend upon the
victory at Yorktown : —

"HEAD-QUARTERS AT THE ROUND O, 10 Dec. 1781.

"MY DEAR FRIEND, — Your favor of the 1st November has just
come to hand. Whatever sweet things may be said of me, there
are not less said of you. Colonel Lee, who lately returned from
the Northern army, says you are the genius of it, and that every
thing is said of you that you can wish. I will not wound your deli-
cacy by repeating his remarks. Your success in Virginia is brilliant,
glorious, great, and important. The Commander-in-chief's head is
all covered with laurels, and yours so shaded with them that one can
hardly get sight of it.

"I long to be with you, our spirits are congenial and our principles and sentiments the same. A long distance separates, and
alas ! I fear, with you, we shall not have a happy meeting for a long
time to come. But be assured my esteem and affection are neither
lessened by time nor distance ; and I hope at some future day, when
the cannon shall cease to roar, and the olive-branch appears, we
shall experience a happy meeting. Your great success in Virginia

gives me the most flattering hopes that this winter will terminate the war.

" P.S. — Don't be surprised if you hear I attempt the siege of Charleston ; nor must you be disappointed greatly, should we fail."

In March, 1782, Knox and Gouverneur Morris were appointed commissioners to arrange a cartel for a general exchange of prisoners ; to liquidate the expenses of their maintenance ; and to provide for their subsistence in future.

They met the British Commissioners — General William Dalrymple, whom Knox had formerly known as commander of the 14th Regiment in Boston, and Andrew Elliot, Esq. — at Elizabethtown, N.J., on the 30th ; but the differences upon essential points were so great, no arrangement could be effected, notwithstanding the earnest and persevering exertions of the American agents. They transmitted the account of their proceedings to Washington, who thus replied : —

" I should do injustice to my own feelings on this occasion if I did not express something beyond my bare approbation of the attention, address, and ability exhibited by you, gentlemen, in the course of this tedious and fruitless negotiation. The want of succeeding in the great object of your mission does not, however, lessen in my estimation the merit which is due to the unwearied assiduity for the public good, and the benevolent zeal to alleviate the distresses of the unfortunate, which seem to have actuated you on every occasion, and for which, I entreat, you will be pleased to accept my most cordial thanks."

In the following letter to Washington, Knox refers to the obstacles the commissioners had encountered, and acknowledges his obligations to him for his promotion as a major-general, which took place on the 22d of March, 1782, dating from 15 November, 1781 : —

"BASKENRIDGE, 21 April, 1782.

"We have at last left Elizabethtown.   Our stay there was unreasonably protracted by the frequent references to New York.

"We have very good reason to believe that all the important propositions made by us were discussed in New York by a council of general officers. . . . Every circumstance we observed tended to convince us that we never shall obtain justice or equal treatment from the enemy but when [we are] in a situation to demand it.

. . . "Your Excellency knows the importance and value of the intelligence you obtain through the medium of Elizabethtown. In my opinion, nothing but the importance of this would counterbalance the evils which arise from continuing a post there. If all exchanges of prisoners were made by the North River, it would be better, and prevent much improper communication, which unavoidably prevails at present.

"I have received a letter from General Lincoln, informing that Congress have been pleased to promote me in the manner most flattering to my wishes, founded upon your Excellency's letter from Yorktown.

"I cannot express how deeply I am impressed with a sense of your kindness, and the favorable point of view in which you have regarded my feeble attempts to promote the service of my country. I shall ever retain, my dear General, a lively sense of your goodness and friendship, and shall be happy indeed if my future conduct shall meet with your approbation."

In July, Knox, who had been inspecting the fortifications of West Point, informed Washington by letter of its inability to stand a siege, and of the deficiencies in its magazines, buildings, &c.; and, on being appointed to the command of that post on Aug. 29, set himself vigorously at work to strengthen and complete the works.   In his letter of instructions, Washington thus evinces his appreciation of Knox: "I have so thorough a confidence in you, and so well am I acquainted with your abilities and activity, that I think it needless to point out to you the great outlines of your duty."

The discontent of the army respecting the arrearages of its pay was increased by the prospect of its being ere long disbanded, without adequate provision by Congress for a settlement; and it manifested itself in audible murmurs and complaints, which threatened serious consequences.

In December, 1782, a committee of officers was chosen to draft an address and petition to Congress. This was drawn up by Knox, its chairman, and contained a statement of the amounts due them; a proposal that the half-pay for life should be commuted for a specific sum; and a request that security should be given by the government for the fulfilment of its engagements.

General McDougall, with Colonels Brooks and Ogden, were deputed to bear this memorial to Congress, which body, in January, 1783, passed resolves concerning it, indefinite in their character and unsatisfactory to the officers. The disappointment and irritation felt at this result produced the famous "Newburg Addresses," by which the feelings of the officers were wrought up to the highest pitch.

At this point the strenuous exertions of Knox were joined with those of Washington, in composing the discontented and mutinous spirit which appeared; and at the meeting of officers held March 15th, at which Washington by a patriotic and impressive address allayed the storm which threatened the peace of the country, Knox moved the resolutions thanking him for the course he had pursued and expressive of their unabated attachment, and also declaring their unshaken reliance on the good faith of Congress and their country, and a determination to bear with patience their grievances till, in due time, they should be redressed. The subject was again considered in Congress, and the commutation and other provisions asked for in the memorial were granted.

The extracts from Knox's letters, given below, present a faithful picture of his sentiments and those of the army upon this subject, and upon the still more important one, — a stronger and more responsible government.

TO GENERAL LINCOLN.

"20 Dec. 1782.

" I am, and I believe the whole army are, perfectly in sentiment with you respecting a commutation of half-pay. The accounts up to the present period ought to be settled by somebody. The State settlement for the reasons you have given must be preferable. The expectations of the army, from the drummer to the highest officers, are so.keen for *some* pay, that I shudder at the idea of their not receiving it. The utmost period of sufferance upon that head has arrived. To attempt to lengthen it will undoubtedly occasion commotions. The gentlemen sent with the address have been unable to raise the money for their expenses, until yesterday. The army will have anxious moments until they shall know the result."

TO GOUVERNEUR MORRIS.

"21 Feb. 1783.

" The army generally have always reprobated the idea of being thirteen armies. Their ardent desires have been to be one continental body looking up to one sovereign. This would have prevented much heart-burning at the partialities which have been practised by the respective States. They know of no way of bringing this about, at a period when peace appears to be in full view. Certain it is they are good patriots, and would forward any thing that would tend to produce union, and a permanent general constitution; . . . but they must be directed in the mode by the proper authority.

" It is a favorite toast in the army, 'A hoop to the barrel,' or ' Cement to the Union.' America will have fought and bled to little purpose if the powers of government shall be insufficient to preserve the peace, and this must be the case without general funds. As the present Constitution is so defective, why do not you great men call the people together and tell them so ; that is, to have a convention of the States to form a better Constitution ? This appears to us,

11

who have a superficial view only, to be the more efficacious remedy. Let something be done before a peace takes place, or we shall be in a worse situation than we were at the commencement of the war."

TO GENERAL M^CDOUGALL.

"WEST POINT, 21 Feb. 1783.

"I received the report signed by you and Colonel Ogden, copies of which have been distributed to the different parts of the army. The business, instead of being brought to a close, seems more remote from a decision than it was before the application to Congress. The complex system of government operates most powerfully in the present instance against the army, who certainly deserve every thing in the power of a grateful people to give.

"We are in an unhappy predicament indeed, not to know who are responsible to us for a settlement of accounts.

"Posterity will hardly believe that an army contended incessantly for eight years under a constant pressure of misery to establish the liberties of their country, without knowing who were to compensate them or whether they were ever to receive any reward for their services. It is high time that we should, now we have a prospect of peace, know whether the respective States or the whole, aggregately, are to recognize our dues and to place them upon such principles as to promise some future benefit. Much has been said about the influence of the army : . . . it can only exist in one point, that to be sure is a sharp point, which I hope in God will never be directed but against the enemies of the liberties of America. . . .

"It will take much time to change or amend the present form [of government]: must our accounts, therefore, remain unsettled until this shall have been considered and decided upon? I think not.

"My sentiments are exactly these. I consider the reputation of the American army as one of the most immaculate things on earth, and that we should even suffer wrongs and injuries to the utmost verge of toleration rather than sully it in the least degree. But there is a point beyond which there is no sufferance. I pray sincerely we may not pass it. . . . I have not taken the sense of the army upon your report; that is, I have not called any number of officers together upon this subject, because, as no decision has been made, nothing they can say will, in the least, forward the matter. I ardently wish you may be able to fix the rate of commutation, and have a person appointed to settle the accounts of the army, and then have a reference to the respective States, to become responsible for the sums which may be found due upon both principles of accounts and commutation of half-pay.   .

"You will readily perceive I mean this as a private letter, nay, more, a *confidential* one."

TO THE SAME.

" WEST POINT, 3 March, 1783.

"The army are impatiently waiting the result of your mission. I earnestly wish it may produce more than it at present seems to promise. I am certain nothing is wanting on your part to bring the matter to a happy termination. It is enough to sicken one to observe how light a matter many States make of their not being represented in Congress, — a good proof of the badness of the present Constitution.

"Your view of the sentiments of the people on a prospect of peace is a just representation of what we are to expect after that event. However, let them first do the army justice, and we shall demand a very small pittance of their gratitude, and little shall we find it.

To McDougall he again writes on the 12th, two days after the appearance of the " Newburg Addresses : "—

"I sincerely hope we shall not be influenced to actions which may be contrary to our uniform course of service for eight years. The men who, by their illiberality and injustice drive the army to the very brink of destruction, ought to be punished with severity.

"The measures we can take to remedy our evils are not known to me. I know not how by any violence we can obtain a settlement of accounts, and have the half-pay placed upon proper principles, except by the applications we have made. Endeavor, my dear friend, once more to convince the obdurate of the awful evils which may arise from postponing a decision on the subjects of our address."

TO GENERAL LINCOLN.

" WEST POINT, 3 March, 1783.

"I most earnestly conjure you to urge that every thing respecting the army be decided upon before peace takes place. No time ought to be lost. Let the public only comply with their own promises, and the army will return to their respective homes the lambs and bees of the community. But if they should be disbanded previous to a settlement, without knowing who to look to for an adjustment of accounts and a responsibility of payment, they will be so deeply stung by the injustice and ingratitude of their country as to become its tigers and wolves."

And again, on the 12th : —   .

"The officers are waiting impatiently the result of General McDougall's mission. Their impatience is almost heightened into despair. Papers have been distributed by unknown persons, calling the body of the officers together yesterday in the new building, accompanied by an address calculated to rouse the officers to redress their own grievances. The Commander-in-chief requested that the meeting might be postponed until next Saturday. What will be the result, God only knows. Congress ought not to lose a moment in bringing the affairs of the army to a decision. Push the matter instantly, my dear sir, with all your might and main."

On the 16th he writes : —

"The meeting was had yesterday. The occasion, though intended for opposite purposes, has been one of the happiest circumstances of the war, and will set the military character of America in a high point of view. If the people have the most latent spark of gratitude, this generous proceeding of the army must call it forth. For these reasons, I think the proceedings ought to be published. Can you not have this done immediately? If so, forward some hundred copies to the army. The General's address is a masterly performance."

It was at this time that Knox, in order to perpetuate the friendships formed by the officers of the army, so soon to be disbanded, and at the same time to create a fund for their indigent widows and orphans, founded the Society of the Cincinnati, each officer upon joining contributing to its treasury one month's pay. Washington was chosen its President, and Knox Secretary; and the French admirals, generals, and colonels who had served in America were also constituted members.

Its Institution, which was the work of Knox, was carried into effect, with some slight amendments, in May, 1783. One of its features aroused considerable hostility, and gave rise to much discussion. This was the provision by which the eldest male heir succeeded to a vacant membership, and which was vehemently assailed as introducing an order of nobility into the republic. Time has refuted the calumnies to which the Society was subjected; and its career of beneficence, still active, testifies to the wisdom as well as to the benevolence of its founder. Knox continued its secretary until the year 1800, and in 1805 became vice-president. He was also vice-president of the Massachusetts branch in 1783.

Knox had been left by Washington in command of the army on August 26, and in November he began the delicate and arduous task of disbanding it. The evacuation of New York by the enemy gave rise to the following correspondence between the respective commanders: —

WASHINGTON TO KNOX.

"ROCKY HILL, 23 Oct. 1783.

" The arrival of the definitive treaty and the evacuation of New York have been so long delayed as to interfere very materially with our arrangements for the celebration of peace. . . . I think, therefore, that it will be best to defer it until the British leave the city, and then to have it at that place, where all who choose to attend can find accommodation.

" Sir Guy Carleton some time since informed me, through Mr. Parker, that he should leave New York, in all, next month, probably by the 20th; and that when the transports which were gone to Nova Scotia returned, he should be able to fix the day. This

notice may be short; and, as it is best to be prepared, I wish you to
confer on the subject with Governor Clinton, and have every necessary arrangement made for taking possession of the city on their
leaving it. You will please to report to me the arrangements you
may agree on.

"Enclosed I transmit you copy of a proclamation of Congress for
the dissolution of the army: you will please to publish it to the
troops under your orders."

KNOX TO SIR GUY CARLETON.

"WEST POINT, 9 Nov. 1783.

"SIR, — By your Excellency's verbal message, transmitted
through Mr. Parker to his Excellency General Washington, expressing your expectations of being able to withdraw his Brittanic
Majesty's troops from New York in the course of the present month;
and by recent reports from there, it appears probable that the period
is fixed for that event. In this case, I flatter myself your Excellency will see how necessary it may be for the protection of the
city and its inhabitants, that it should be immediately occupied by
some American forces. I have received his Excellency General
Washington's directions on this head, and I have consulted with his
Excellency Governor Clinton, who is too unwell to take any measures himself, but is exceedingly desirous that every arrangement
should be made which would induce to good order until the civil
authority of the State should be established.

"Having the command of the military in this quarter, and being
assured of your Excellency's perfect disposition to insure the safety
of the city, I have taken the liberty to address you upon this point,
and to request the honor that you would favor me in season with
the information of the precise time when you may please to relinquish the jurisdiction of the posts now in your possession, as the
troops for the before-mentioned purpose would principally be drawn
from the neighborhood of this post. I hope it will be a sufficient
apology for requesting five or six days' notice previous to the em-
barkation of the last of your corps.

"Captain Lillie, my aide-de-camp, will have the honor to deliver
this letter and receive your Excellency's answer."

"NEW YORK, 12 Nov. 1783.

"SIR, — I have this day communicated to his Excellency General Washington, by letter, my intention of relinquishing the posts at King's Bridge and as far as McGowan's Pass, inclusive, on this Island on the 21st instant; to resign the possession of Herrick's and Hampstead with all to the eastward on Long Island, on the same day; and, if possible, to give up this city with Brooklyn on the day following, and Paulus Hook, Dennys's, and Staten Island as soon after as may be practicable, reserving only with respect to New York that, if any of our ships should happen to want repairs after the town is evacuated, we shall still have the free and uninterrupted use of the Ship Yard, under the direction of such officer as the Admiral shall appoint, as long as it may be requisite for that purpose.

"Major Beckwith, my oldest aide-de-camp, who waits upon you with this letter, will communicate such other particulars as may be necessary for your further information."

On the 25th of November the British army evacuated the city; and Knox, at the head of the American troops, took possession. The principal officers of the army yet remaining in service assembled, on Dec. 4, at Fraunce's Tavern to take a final leave of their beloved chief. Washington entered the room where they were all waiting, and taking a glass of wine in his hand he said, "With a heart full of love and gratitude I now take leave of you. I most devoutly wish that your latter days may be as prosperous and happy as your former ones have been glorious and honorable." Having drunk, he continued: "I cannot come to each of you to take my leave, but shall be obliged to you if each will come and take me by the hand." Knox who stood nearest to him turned and grasped his hand; and while the tears flowed down the cheeks of each, the Commander-in-chief kissed him. This he did to each of his officers, while tears and sobs stifled utterance.

Upon his return to West Point, Dec. 18th, Knox was officially thanked by Governor Clinton and the Council for his attention to the rights of the citizens of the State of New York, and for his zeal in preserving peace and good order since the evacuation.

The following letter to Washington explains itself : —

"WEST POINT, 29 Sept. 1783.

"SIR, — I beg leave to state to your Excellency, and through you to the honorable Congress, that the unavoidable expenses arising from the command of this post and its dependencies have greatly exceeded any emoluments of office arising from my rank in the army ; and that, in order to support my station with some propriety, so as not to reflect disgrace upon the public rank I sustain, I have been obliged to make use of my private resources to a considerable amount.

"That it has uniformly been customary, from the peculiar expenses of the command, to allow the emoluments of a major-general commanding in a separate department, and that said allowance was withdrawn a short time previous to your Excellency's ordering me on the command. It may be unnecessary to enter into a detail of circumstances which have rendered my command as expensive as that of my predecessors. It is sufficient that I can easily prove that it has been so. I therefore honestly hope to have the same compensation.

"I pray that your Excellency would have the goodness to place this request before Congress in the manner that you may think it deserves."

In consequence of this application, Congress, on the 30th of October, allowed him the pay of a major-general in a separate department, during his command at West Point. This gave him an additional sum of ninety dollars per month from Sept. 1st, 1782, amounting to $1,350. He retained command of that post until early in January, 1784.

With Washington he continued to keep up an active

correspondence, which terminated only with the death of his chief, whose efforts were not wanting when, as in the present case, it seemed likely that they could be of service to his friend who desired to continue to serve his country in the capacity in which he could be most useful.

KNOX TO WASHINGTON.

"WEST POINT, 17 Sept. 1783.

"MY DEAR GENERAL, — I cannot refrain from communicating the joy I feel, and the pleasure manifested by the officers in general, upon the noble testimony of gratitude exhibited by Congress in their resolve concerning the Equestrian Statue. This permanent evidence of their sense of your services will illustrate their virtue and honor more than whole columns of panegyric.

"I am daily solicited for information respecting the progress of the officers' petition for a new State westward of the Ohio. . . . Were the prayer of the petition to be granted, the officers in a very few years would make the finest settlement on the frontiers, and form a strong barrier against the barbarians.

"I have had it in contemplation for a long time past, to mention to your Excellency the idea of a *master general* of ordnance. But I hesitated, and finally declined it in my last opinion to you upon a peace establishment, lest it might be concluded that I was endeavoring to create a post for myself. But the resignation of the minister of war eventual upon the definitive treaty of peace, and his opinion that no successor will be appointed, joined to the necessity of having some person responsible to Congress, seem to combine to render such an officer peculiarly necessary, who should principally reside near Congress to execute orders as they should think proper for the dignity or security of the republic. It is a well-known fact that so complex and extensive a business as the formation of an ordnance and its numerous dependencies, the manufacture of small arms and accoutrements, must be the work of much time, and can only be effectually prepared in profound peace.

"Congress have evinced so much wisdom and magnanimity in their conduct, that it cannot be doubted that they will make the most substantial arrangements for future exigencies consistent with their revenues and the nicest economy.

12

"The abundant experience I have had of your Excellency's kindness and friendship has induced me to communicate this in confidence. I beg leave at the same time to remark, that, although my expectations and wishes are for private life, yet if any office similar to the above should be formed upon the broad scale of national policy, I might, if thought worthy, find it convenient to give it my zealous assistance. I mention this matter more readily from a remembrance of your favorable recommendations for the office of Secretary at War."

WASHINGTON TO KNOX.

"ROCKY HILL, 2d Nov. 1783.

" General Lincoln's resignation has been offered, and accepted by Congress. . . . I have conversed with several members of Congress upon the propriety, in time of peace, of uniting the offices of Secretary at War and Master of Ordnance in one person, and letting him have the command of the troops on the peace establishment, not as an appendage of right, — for that I think would be wrong, — but by separate appointment at the discretion of Congress. Those I have spoken to on the subject seem to approve the idea, which, if adopted, would make a handsome appointment. I will converse with others on this head, and let you know the result. My wishes to serve you in it you need not doubt, being with much truth

" Your most affectionate
" GEORGE WASHINGTON."

KNOX TO WASHINGTON.

" WEST POINT, 3d Jan. 1784.

. . . "I have discharged all the troops but those specified in the enclosed return. I believe I did not mention to your Excellency my ideas of the pay for the offices that might be associated; viz., the duties of the Secretary at War, Master of Ordnance, and charge or command of any troops which might be retained in service. It appears to me, and I hope that I fairly estimate the expenses and trouble, that the pay and emoluments of a major-general in a separate department free of any encumbrances would not be an unreasonable appointment. Should Congress think proper to honor me with an offer of these offices associated together, I should be willing to accept them upon the above terms; but I

should do injustice to myself and family to accept of any employment which would not prevent my involving myself.

"Having brought the affairs here nearly to a close, I shall soon
depart for Boston, for which place Mrs. Knox and her little family
set out from New York on the 10th ult. I should do violence to
the dictates of my heart were I to suppress its sensations of affection and gratitude to you for the innumerable instances of your
kindness and attention to me. And, although I can find no words
equal to their warmth, I may venture to assure you that they will
remain indelibly fixed. I devoutly pray the Supreme Being to continue to afford you his especial protection."

In January, 1784, Knox arrived at Boston, and took up
his residence in Dorchester.*

With General Lincoln and George Partridge he was in
June appointed by the General Court of Massachusetts a
commissioner to treat with the Penobscot Indians, in order
to induce them to relinquish their lands from the head of
the tide forty miles up the river. They were also instructed to examine whether the people under the government of Nova Scotia had encroached upon the territories
of Massachusetts, and to settle the Eastern boundary line,
a dispute having arisen as to which was the river St. Croix
intended by the treaty with Great Britain. The commissioners having performed the duty assigned them made
their report a few months later.

From Paris La Fayette writes to Knox on Jan. 8,
1784 : —

"It has been to me a great happiness to hear from you; and while
we are separated, I beg you will let me enjoy it as often as possible.
You know my tender affection for you, my dear Knox, is engraved

---

* The house in which Knox lived may still be seen a short distance
beyond the Second Congregational Church, on the upper road to Milton. It
was formerly owned by a Mr. Jones. It has long been the property of the
Welles family, bankers of Boston and Paris, and was for one or more years
the summer residence of Daniel Webster.

in my heart, and I shall keep it as long as I live. From the beginning of our great Revolution, which has been the beginning of our
acquaintance, we have been actuated by the same principles, impressed with the same ideas, attached to the same friends, and we
have warmly loved and confidentially intrusted each other. The
remembrance of all this is dear to my heart; and from every motive
of tenderness and regard, I set the greater value by the happiness
of your possession as a bosom friend. I have been much employed
in rendering America what service I could in the affairs of her
commerce. What I can do must be entirely done before the spring,
when I intend embarking for my beloved shores of Liberty. My
delays in Europe are owing to motives of American public service. . . . Dunkirk, L'Orient, Bayonne, and Marseilles have been
declared free ports of America."

When the gallant Frenchman visited Boston in October,
1784, he was met at Watertown, on the 15th, by a number
of the officers of the late continental army, headed by
Knox; and together they sat down to an elegant repast
provided for the occasion. On the following day he was
waited on by them with an address by Knox, to which the
marquis made a suitable reply. A more general welcome
was extended by the citizens on the 19th, when a public
dinner was given in his honor, at Faneuil Hall, at which
many persons of distinction, among them seventy-five
officers of the Revolutionary army, were present.

Congress having, on March 4, 1785, fixed the salary of
the Secretary of War for the future at $2,450, proceeded
on the 8th to elect Knox to that office. He thus replies
to the letter of the Secretary notifying him of his election : —

TO CHARLES THOMSON, ESQ., SECRETARY OF CONGRESS.

"BOSTON, 17 March, 1785.

"SIR, — I have had the pleasure to receive your favor of the
9th instant, informing of the honor conferred on me by the

United States in Congress assembled, in electing me Secretary of War, and enclosing the ordinance for ascertaining the powers and duties of the office, the act establishing the salary, and the minute of the election.

" I have the most grateful sentiments to Congress for this distinguishing mark of their confidence ; and I shall, according to the best of my abilities, attempt to execute the duties of the office. I shall have a perfect reliance upon a candid interpretation of my actions, and I shall hope that application to business and propriety of intention may, in a degree, excuse a deficiency of talents.

" My affairs here will require my personal attention the latter end of May and beginning of June, and I hope to be indulged with a few weeks' absence at that time, provided it can be granted without public injury. In the mean time, I shall endeavor to be at New York about the 12th of next month."

And from Boston he wrote to Washington on the 24th, acquainting him with his appointment, from which letter we extract as follows : —

" You may probably have heard that Congress have been pleased to appoint me Secretary at War. I have accepted the appointment, and shall expect to be in New York about the 15th of next month. From the habits imbibed during the war, and from the opinion of my friends that I should make but an indifferent trader, I thought, upon mature consideration, that it was well to accept it, although the salary would be but a slender support. I have dependence upon an unwieldy estate of Mrs. Knox's family, and upon the public certificates given for my services; but neither of these is productive, and require a course of years to render them so. In the mean time, my expenses are considerable, and require some funds for their supply. Congress have rendered the powers and duties of the office respectable; and the circumstances of my appointment, without solicitation on my part, were flattering, nine States out of eleven voting for me. I do not expect to move my family to New York until June next."

Washington in reply, under date of June 18th, says: " Without a compliment, I think a better choice could not have been made."

It is impossible to read without emotion the following lines from a letter written by General Greene a short time before his death, which occurred on June 19th. It bears Knox's indorsement: "This is the last letter I ever received from my truly beloved friend, General Greene." The first paragraph refers to two pieces of cannon presented to him by order of Congress, upon which Knox had caused appropriate inscriptions to be engraved. Its closing request received Knox's earnest and friendly attention: —

"MULBERRY GROVE, 12 March, 1786.

"I thank you for the polite attention you are paying to my public trophies; but I have been so embarrassed and perplexed in my private affairs for a long time past, which originated in the progress of the war, that I have but little spirit or pleasure on such subjects. My family is in distress, and I am overwhelmed with difficulties; and God knows when or where they will end. I work hard and live poor, but I fear all this will not extricate me. . . . Please to give me your opinion upon sending George [his son] to the Marquis La Fayette, agreeable to his request. Let your answer be as candid as I trust your friendship is sincere."

The disturbances in Massachusetts having assumed a serious aspect, in October we find Knox at Springfield, providing for the security of the arsenal there. To a request from General Shepard of the State militia for permission to use the arms and stores of the United States there collected, Knox replies on Jan. 27, 1787, that in case the insurgents should demonstrate an intention of seizing the arsenal or any of the stores, and it could not otherwise be successfully defended, "part might be taken for the protection of the remainder, to be returned the instant the danger should subside."

With Washington, Rufus King, Stephen Higginson, General Lincoln, Nathaniel Gorham, and other prominent Federalists, he kept up an active correspondence; and in the letters which follow he describes vividly the state of feeling in Massachusetts, during the period of Shays's insurrection, the formation of the Federal Constitution and its adoption by that State, a period of intense excitement, especially to one possessing his ardent temper and strong convictions upon the great questions at issue.

TO WASHINGTON.

"NEW YORK, 23 Oct. 1786.

. . . "I have lately been far eastward of Boston on private business, and was no sooner returned here than the commotions in Massachusetts hurried me back to Boston on a public account.

"Our political machine, composed of thirteen independent sovereignties, have been perpetually operating against each other and against the federal head ever since the peace. The powers of Congress are totally inadequate to preserve the balance between the respective States, and oblige them to do those things which are essential for their own welfare or for the general good. The frame of mind in the local legislatures seems to be exerted to prevent the federal constitution from having any good effect. The machine works inversely to the public good in all its parts: not only is State against State, and all against the federal head, but the States within themselves possess the name only without having the essential concomitant of government, the power of preserving the peace, the protection of the liberty and property of the citizens. On the very first impression of faction and licentiousness, the fine theoretic government of Massachusetts has given way, and its laws [are] trampled under foot. Men at a distance, who have admired our systems of government unfounded in nature, are apt to accuse the rulers, and say that taxes have been assessed too high and collected too rigidly. This is a deception equal to any that has been hitherto entertained. That taxes may be the ostensible cause is true, but that they are the true cause is as far remote from truth as light from darkness. The people who are the insurgents have never paid any or but very little taxes. But they see the weakness of government: they feel at once their own poverty compared with the opulent, and their own force, and they are determined to make use of the latter in order to remedy the former.

"Their creed is, that the property of the United States has been

protected from the confiscations of Britain by the joint exertions of
all, and therefore ought to be the common property of all; and he
that attempts opposition to this creed is an enemy to equality and
justice, and ought to be swept from the face of the earth. In a
word, they are determined to annihilate all debts public and private,
and have agrarian laws, which are easily effected by the means of
unfunded paper money, which shall be a tender in all cases whatever. The numbers of these people may amount, in Massachusetts,
to one-fifth part of several populous counties; and to them may be
added the people of similar sentiments from the States of Rhode
Island, Connecticut, and New Hampshire, so as to constitute a body
of twelve or fifteen thousand desperate and unprincipled men. They
are chiefly of the young and active part of the community, more
easily collected than kept together afterwards. But they will probably commit overt acts of treason, which will compel them to embody
for their own safety. Once embodied, they will be constrained to
submit to discipline for the same reason.

"Having proceeded to this length, for which they are now ripe,
we shall have a formidable rebellion against reason, the principle of
all government, and against the very name of liberty.

"This dreadful situation, for which our government have made
no adequate provision, has alarmed every man of principle and property in New England. They start as from a dream, and ask what
can have been the cause of our delusion? What is to give us
security against the violence of lawless men? Our government
must be braced, changed, or altered to secure our lives and property.
We imagined that the mildness of our government and the wishes
of the people were so correspondent that we were not as other
nations, requiring brutal force to support the laws.

"But we find that we are men, — actual men, possessing all the
turbulent passions belonging to that animal, and that we must have
a government proper and adequate for him.

"The people of Massachusetts, for instance, are far advanced in
this doctrine, and the men of property and the men of station and
principle there are determined to endeavor to establish and protect
them in their lawful pursuits; and, what will be efficient in all cases
of internal commotions or foreign invasions, they mean that liberty shall form the basis, — liberty resulting from an equal and firm
administration of law.

" They wish for a general government of unity, as they see that the local legislatures must naturally and necessarily tend to retard the general government. We have arrived at that point of time in which we are forced to see our own humiliation, as a nation, and that a progression in this line cannot be productive of happiness, private or public. Something is wanting, and something must be done, or we shall be involved in all the horror of failure, and civil war without a prospect of its termination. Every friend to the liberty of his country is bound to reflect, and step forward to prevent the dreadful consequences which shall result from a government of events. Unless this is done, we shall be liable to be ruled by an arbitrary and capricious armed tyranny, whose word and will must be law.

" The Indians on our frontiers are giving indisputable evidence of their hostile intentions. Congress, anxiously desirous of meeting the evils on the frontiers, have unanimously agreed to augment the troops now in service to a legionary corps of 2,040 men. This measure is important, and will tend to strengthen the principles of government, if necessary, as well as to defend the frontiers. I mention the idea of strengthening government as confidential. But the State of Massachusetts requires the greatest assistance, and Congress are fully impressed with the importance of supporting her with great exertions."

TO STEPHEN HIGGINSON.

"NEW YORK, 28th Jan. 1787.

" The zeal of the people of Boston and the lower country in favor of government is a good sign, and will probably produce the results expected from it. But, supposing the present disorders quieted, some measures will be necessary to prevent a repetition of them. Although the patriotism of individuals may restore [to] government its former tone, some more certain principle than zeal will be requisite to retain it. Massachusetts, by an exertion in the present instance, may even acquire a temporary vigor; but the poor, poor federal government is sick almost unto death. .

" But one feeble sign of life for upwards of two, almost three months past. No Congress but for part of one day. How things are to be worked up so as to produce by its ordinary operations a remedy for the numerous existing disorders, or be made adequate to

13

the great purposes of a nation, which, considering its vast resources, ought to be a dignified one, it is difficult, if not impossible, to conjecture.

"A convention is proposed by Virginia, and acceded to by Pennsylvania, Jersey, probably New York and South Carolina, to consult on some plan to prevent our utter ruin. Perhaps this convention originated, and has been imbued with ideas, far short of a radical reform. Let this have been the case, may it notwithstanding be turned to an excellent purpose? Our views are limited in all things, we can only see from point to point at a time. If men — great men — are sent to the convention, might they not assist the vision of the Southern delegates in such a manner as to induce the adoption of some energetic plan, in the prosecution of which we might rise to national dignity and happiness?

"Should the convention agree on some continental constitution, and propose the great outlines, either through Congress, or directly to their constituents, the respective legislatures, with a request that State conventions might be assembled for the sole purpose of choosing delegates to a continental convention in order to consider and decide upon a general government, and to publish it for general observance in the same manner as Congress formed and decided upon the articles of confederation and perpetual union, would not this, to all intents and purposes, be a government derived from the people and assented to by them as much as they assented to the confederation? If it be not the best mode, is it not the best which is practicable? If so, one would conclude that it ought to be embraced.

"The Southern States are jealous enough already. If New England, and particularly Massachusetts, should decline sending delegates to the convention, it will operate in a duplicate ratio to injure us by annihilating the rising desire in the Southern States of effecting a better national system, and by adding to their jealousies of the designs of New England.

"I have dwelt on this subject to you, in order that if your sentiments should correspond with mine, that you should influence a choice of delegates of such characters as would possess the ability of pointing out the road to national glory and felicity."

TO GENERAL LINCOLN.

"NEW YORK, 14 Feb. 1787.

" While I thank you for your kind communication of the 5th inst., I most heartily congratulate you on the successful events contained therein [the suppression of the Shays] insurrection. Were not your military reputation already highly established, your manœuvres would have elevated it; but, circumstanced as you are in the opinion of your friends and the world, Shays's rebellion is not a field in which you could gather fresh laurels. It will be a sufficient satisfaction to you that you have dissipated a cloud that threatened a violent storm.

" The convention proposed by the commercial convention last September, to meet in Philadelphia in May next, engrosses a great portion of the attention of the men of reflection. Some are for and some against it; but the preponderance of opinion is for it. None of the New England States have yet chosen, and it appears quite problematical whether any will choose unless Massachusetts. The convention will be at liberty to consider more diffusively the defects of the present system than Congress can, who are the executors of a certain system. If what they should think proper to propose, after mature deliberation, should require the assent of the people of the respective States, which is supposed necessary in an original compact, the convention would recommend to the respective legislatures to call State conventions for the sole purpose of choosing delegates to represent them in a continental convention, in order to consider and finally decide on a general constitution, and to publish the same for observance. If a differently constructed republican government should be the object, the shortest road to it will be found to be the convention. I hope, therefore, that Massachusetts will choose, and that you, Mr. King, and Mr. Higginson should be three of the delegates."

TO RUFUS KING.

"NEW YORK, 15th July, 1787.

" I am happy the convention continue together without agitating the idea of adjournment. If their attempts should prove inadequate to effect capital alterations, yet experience will be gained, which may serve important purposes on another occasion.

"The conduct of France in establishing provincial assemblies is seized with great eagerness by the advocates for the State systems, as a reason against any alterations. But they do not bring into view the strong cement of the royal authority supported by 200,000 soldiers.

"The State systems are the accursed thing which will prevent our being a nation. The democracy might be managed, nay, it would remedy itself after being sufficiently fermented; but the vile State governments are sources of pollution, which will contaminate the American name perhaps for ages. Machines that must produce ill, but cannot produce good, smite them in the name of God and the people.

"Eight States in Congress, — they yesterday passed with great unanimity a system of government for the western territory."

TO LA FAYETTE.

"NEW YORK, 24 Oct. 1787.

"You will have received, long before this period, the result of the convention which assembled in Philadelphia during the month of May. These propositions being essentially different in many respects from the existing confederation, and which will probably produce different national effects, are contemplated by the public at large with an anxious attention. The discussions are commenced in the newspapers and in pamphlets, with all the freedom and liberality which characterize a people who are searching, by their own experience, after a form of government most productive of happiness. To speak decisively at this moment of the fate of the proposed constitution, characterizes effectually the person giving the opinion. Habituated as I have been for a long time to desire the consolidation of the powers of all parts of this country, as an indispensable requisite to national character and national happiness, I receive the propositions as they are, and from my soul I wish them God speed! The transition from wishing an event, to believing that it will happen, is easy indeed. I therefore am led to a strong persuasion that the proposed government will be generally or universally adopted in the course of twelve or fifteen months.

"In desiring that the proposed government may be adopted, I would not have you believe that I think it all perfect. There are several things in it that I confess I could wish to see altered. But

I apprehend no alterations can be effected peaceably. All the States represented agreed to the constitution as it stands. There are substantial reasons to believe that such an agreement could not again be produced even by the same men."

TO WASHINGTON.

"NEW YORK, 14 Jan. 1788.

"The Massachusetts convention were to meet on the 9th. The decision of Connecticut will influence, in a degree, their determination, and I have no doubt the constitution will be adopted; but it is at this moment questionable whether with a large majority. There are three parties existing in that State at present, not exceedingly different in their respective numbers, but greatly differing in wealth and ability.

"The first is the commercial part of the State, to whom are added all the men of considerable property, the clergy, the lawyers, including all the judges of all the courts; and all the officers of the late army, and the neighborhood of all the great towns, are of this party. Its strength in point of numbers may include three-sevenths of the whole State. This party are for the most vigorous government. Perhaps many of them would have been more pleased with the new constitution, had it been still more analogous to the British Constitution.

"The second party are the Eastern part of the State, lying beyond New Hampshire, and formerly the province of Maine. This party are mostly looking toward the erection of a new State; and the majority will adopt or reject the new constitution, as it may facilitate or retard their designs, without much regard to the great merits of the question. This party may not be far less than two-sevenths of the State.

"The third party are the insurgents and their favorers, the great majority of whom are for an annihilation of debts, public and private, and therefore cannot approve the new constitution. This party may be more than two-sevenths.

"If the first and second party agree, as will be most probable, and also some of the party stated as in the insurgent interest, the constitution will be adopted by a great majority, notwithstanding all exertions to the contrary.

"Mr. Samuel Adams has declared that he will oppose it, to the

very great disgust of the people of Boston, his constituents. It is
said Boston was about to take some spirited measures to prevent
the effect of his opposition. It is probable the debates will be
lengthy, and that the convention will sit one month before they
decide."

The following from Rufus King to Knox sheds new
light on the history of the adoption of the Federal Constitution in Massachusetts, which event took place on
February 6th. By it we see that the Federalists in the
Convention, under the able leadership of Rufus King and
Theophilus Parsons, secured the support of Governor
Hancock, who also presided over the deliberations of that
body, by an adroit appeal to the special foible of the governor, — vanity. Upon such apparently trivial causes do
the destinies of nations sometimes turn!

" Boston, 3 Feb. 1788.

" DEAR GENERAL, — Hancock has committed himself in our
favor, and will not desert the cause. Saturday's 'Centinel' will
give you an idea of his plan. The Federalists are united in that
system; and, as Adams has joined us on this plan, we are encouraged to think our success is probable.

" Gerry keeps close at Cambridge, and his adherents have made
no motion for his recall. Mr. Hancock's propositions were yesterday committed to a committee of two members from each county:
they meet to-day, and we hope favorably from their deliberations,
a majority being Federalists.

" The final question will probably be taken in five or six days.
You will be astonished, when you see the list of names, that such a
union of men has taken place on this question. Hancock will here-
after receive the universal support of Bowdoin's friends, *and we tell
him that if Virginia does not unite, which is problematical, that he
is considered as the only fair candidate for President."*

In a letter to La Fayette, dated New York, 26 April,
1788, Knox, after reciting the facts and probabilities
respecting the adoption of the Federal Constitution, goes
on to say : —

" As to Rhode Island, no little State of Greece ever exhibited greater turpitude than she does. Paper money and Tender Law engross her attention entirely: this is, in other words, plundering the orphan and widow by virtue of laws.

" Mrs. Greene and her little family you so kindly inquire after are seated at Wethersfield in Connecticut, under the auspices of our friend, Colonel Wadsworth. Mrs. Greene is most honorably and industriously employed in the education of her children. Colonel Wadsworth is anxious George should be sent to France, to which Mrs. Greene consents. It is possible the young gentleman may be addressed to your care in the course of one or two packets hence."

On the 15th of May, he writes to him again upon this subject, as follows : —

" Mr. Barlow of Connecticut, author of the poem entitled the ' Vision of Columbus,' whom I recommend to your kindness, will deliver you this letter, and also he will present to you the son of our late esteemed friend, General Greene.

" I am perfectly impressed with the belief that you will place him in such a situation as will at the same time impress the best morals and the most enlarged information.

" The classics and modern languages, as being the work of memory, will probably constitute his first studies, together with learning the necessary personal exercises to form his manners. Mathematics, geography, astronomy, and the art of drawing will follow of course.

" I flatter myself that, by being entirely removed to a new sphere, he will necessarily imbibe the habits which are in circulation there, and that he will be formed on such a scale as to be an honor to the memory of his father, and the pride of his mother and his other friends.

" His disposition is good, and in my opinion, with a proper education, he promises to make a worthy character : certain I am that under your auspices he will possess the best chances for happiness."

One of his early playmates and friends, Rev. David McClure, writes as follows: —

" EAST WINDSOR, Dec. 22, 1788.

" DEAR SIR, — On the footing of that juvenile friendship and acquaintance with you with which I have been honored, and which was kept alive to our riper years, I now do myself the pleasure to address a line to you, to assure you of my respectful and affectionate remembrance of you, and of the satisfaction with which I sometimes call to mind those scenes of innocent amusement and play in which we were mutually engaged when we were boys.

" I have often thought of our attempts to imitate the man who flew from the steeple of the North Church, by sliding down an oar from the small buildings in your father's house-yard at Wheeler's Point; and by letting fly little wooden men from the garret window on strings. Have you forgotten that diversion?

" I have often rejoiced with gratitude that the Supreme Disposer of all events has preserved you through the dangers you have encountered, and made you so great a blessing to your country, for whose happiness and glory your labors have been directed. May you ever possess that increasing esteem and affection from your country which your services and merits entitle you to.

" I am settled agreeably in this place, five miles from Hartford, in which I have lived more than two years, and to which I removed from my former parish in Hampton, New Hampshire."

To which Knox replies: —

" NEW YORK, 25 Jan. 1789.

" MY DEAR SIR, — Your esteemed favor of the 22d ult. gave me the most sensible pleasure. Our juvenile sports, and the joyful sensations they excited, are fresh in my mind; and what to me renders the remembrance peculiarly precious is, that I always flattered myself that our hearts and minds were similarly constructed.

" Our situations, however, have been widely different. You have been deeply exploring the natural and moral world, in order to impress on the minds of your fellow-mortals their relative connection with the great scale of intelligent being; leading them by all the powers of persuasion to happiness and humble adoration of the

Supreme Head of the universe; while I have been but too much
entangled with the little things of a little globe. But, as it is part
of my belief that we are responsible only for the light we possess,
I hope we have both acted our parts in such a manner as that a
reflection on the past will give us more pleasure than pain, and that
we shall possess a well-grounded hope of a happy immortality.

"My brother William, who is with me, is the only one beside
myself left of my father's family." *

During Knox's career as Secretary of War, Mrs. Knox
was one of the leaders of fashionable society at the seat
of government, and as such attracted considerable notice.
From the manuscript Journal of Dr. Manasseh Cutler,
under date of July 7, 1787, we extract as follows. The
worthy doctor was evidently unaccustomed to the *coiffure*
of the fashionable lady of that day.

"Dined with General Knox [at New York], introduced to his lady
and a French nobleman, Marquis Lotbinière. Several other gentlemen dined with us. Our dinner was served in high style, much in
the French taste. Mrs. Knox is very gross, but her manners are
easy and agreeable. She is sociable, and would be agreeable, were
it not for her affected singularity in dressing her hair. She seems
to mimic the military style, which to me is very disgusting in a
female. Her hair in front is craped at least a foot high, much in
the form of a churn bottom upward, and topped off with a wire
skeleton in the same form, covered with black gauze, which hangs
in streamers down to her back. Her hair behind is a large braid, and
confined with a monstrous crooked comb."

---

* This brother writes from London (26 June, 1783): "I have a very
respectable set of acquaintances in this country as well as in France.
Among the number here is the very respectable and venerable General
Oglethorpe. I passed Sunday and Monday with his family at their country
house. He desired me through you to make his very particular compliments
to General Washington, of whose virtues and talents I have the pleasure to
find he has the highest opinion."

William Knox soon afterward became subject to occasional fits of derange-
ment, and died about 1797.

14

"July 19.

" Dined with General Knox; about forty-four gentlemen, officers of the late continental army, and among them Baron Steuben. General Knox gave us an entertainment in the style of a prince. Every gentleman at the table was of the ' Cincinnati' except myself, and wore his appropriate badge."

Mrs. William S. Smith writes from New York in 1788 to her mother, Mrs. John Adams: —

" General and Mrs. Knox have been very polite and attentive to us. Mrs. Knox is much altered from the character she used to have. She is neat in her dress, attentive to her family, and very fond of her children. But her size is enormous: I am frightened when I look at her; I verily believe that her waist is as large as three of yours at least. The general is not half so fat as he was."

From Griswold's " Republican Court " we take the following : —

" Mrs. Knox had been one of the heroines of the Revolution, nearly as well known in the camp as her husband. She and her husband were, perhaps, the largest couple in the city, and both were favorites, he for really brilliant conversation and unfailing good humor, and she as a lively and meddlesome but amiable leader of society, without whose co-operation it was believed by many besides herself that nothing could be properly done in the drawing-room or the ball-room, or any place indeed where fashionable men and women sought enjoyment. The house of the Secretary was in Broadway, and it was the scene of a liberal and genial hospitality."

Upon the formation of the new government in May, 1789, Knox was continued in his post of War Secretary by Washington.* " To his past services and an unquestioned integrity," says Judge Marshall, " he was admitted to unite a sound understanding ; and the public judgment as well as that of the chief magistrate pronounced him in

* His commission bears date Sept. 12, 1789.

all respects competent to the station he filled." One of his first acts was to provide for his friend, General Lincoln, to whom, on August 4, he wrote as follows: "Although I do not conceive the office of Collector to the Port of Boston adequate to the merits of my friend, yet, as it is the best thing that can be offered at present, I sincerely congratulate you on the appointment."

The framing of a militia system for the country received the early attention of the Secretary. He had, in April, 1783, communicated to Washington his ideas upon this subject, to the effect that there should be a uniform system and annual encampments ; each State to have an arsenal and a sufficient quantity of arms and ammunition ; that the United States should have some troops for the security of the frontiers, and at West Point, "the key to America, which has been so advantageous in the defence of the United States, and is still so important in that view, *as well as of preserving the Union ;*" that a complete system of military education should be formed and adopted ; that there should be three military academies where the United States arsenals are, — one in the Northern, one in the Middle, and one in the Southern States ; and that a code of military laws should be framed and inspectors appointed by Congress, who should annually examine the academies and report to Congress.

Knox's "Plan for the General Arrangement of the Militia of the United States," reported to Congress 18 March, 1786, provided for the embodiment of all male citizens from eighteen to sixty, into three classes, — "The Advanced Corps," "The Main Corps," and "The Reserved Corps ;" the form to be that of the legion ; each legion to consist of 153 commissioned officers and 2,880 non-commissioned officers and privates, and to be commanded by a major-general. The failure of this plan is partly attributable to the unpropitious circumstances of the times.

Of that prepared by him in January, 1790, similar in its general features to the preceding one, his friend, General Lincoln, gave him, at his request, this opinion : —

"Though it would make ours the strongest militia in the world, the people will not adopt it here, if I know Massachusetts. The expense, pay of officers, no pay of men, the burden on masters, calling the youth indiscriminately, disfranchisement for a time in certain cases, officers excluded from actual service, subjection to a draft for a service of three years, &c., will be magnified here, and damn the bill."

Colonel Jackson also informed him that his plan was not very well received in Massachusetts. The opinion of military men abroad seems to have been favorable to Knox's plan, as is seen in this extract from a letter from General Miranda, the South American patriot, whose acquaintance he had made in Boston in 1784 : * —

"LONDON, Feb. 2, 1791.

"I thank you for your estimable letter of the 6th September, 1790, that your brother delivered to me here. I am very happy to see the flourishing state to which North America is grown, and wish that my own poor miserable country in the South could say the same. They can only answer : —

'*Video meliora provoque, deteriora sequor.*'

"I have seen with great pleasure your plan for the establishment of a militia, &c. General Melville, and some other professional men here that have considered the same subject, admired it very much; and I perfectly agree with you, that the form of the Roman Legion

---

* Francisco de Miranda was born in Caracas about 1750. He travelled on foot through a great part of America and Europe ; was a general of division under Dumouriez, in 1792-93 ; was afterward engaged in abortive attempts to shake off the Spanish yoke from his native province, and having been betrayed by Bolivar to the Spaniards ended his days in a dungeon at Cadiz, in 1816.

is infinitely superior to any other organization or military arrangement we know yet."

The legionary formation was for a time adopted as the regular establishment of the United States; but the plan for the militia, though it had the approval of Washington, was not regarded with favor, and a system less onerous as well as less energetic was at length adopted.

The policy to be pursued towards the various Indian tribes of the United States demanded a large share of Knox's attention, and in it he was guided by enlarged and liberal views. In the minutes which he furnished for the President's speech, in October, 1791, he advocates an impartial administration of justice towards them, suggests that the mode of alienating their lands should be properly defined and regulated, and that the advantages of commerce and the blessings of civilization should be extended to them; and that proper penalties should be provided for such lawless persons as shall violate the treaties with them. "A system," he goes on to say, "producing the free operation of the mild principles of religion and benevolence towards an unenlightened race of men would at once be highly economical and honorable to the national character."

A treaty with the Creek Nation of Indians was signed on Aug. 7, 1790, by Knox, as sole commissioner, in behalf of the United States; and by Alexander McGillivray and twenty-three chiefs, in behalf of the Creek nation, by whom an extensive territory claimed by Georgia was relinquished to that State. McGillivray was at the same time commissioned a brigadier-general in the army of the United States.

The unsuccessful expeditions of Harmar in 1790, and of St. Clair in 1791, against the North-western Indians, were followed, in 1794, by the victorious campaign of Wayne, and by the treaty of Greenville in August, 1795, by which peace was established, and the post of Detroit, together with a considerable tract of land, ceded to the United States.

The friends of Jefferson then Secretary of State, and the partisans of the French Revolution, assailed with malignant hostility the administration of Washington; and Knox as its firm supporter, and while the operations against the Indians were yet unsuccessful, came in for a large share of vituperation and calumny. Among the many ardent and devoted friends of Knox was Major Samuel Shaw, a fellow-townsman, and his aide and secretary during the war, and who was deservedly held by him in the highest esteem. " When Major Shaw returned [from a foreign voyage], in 1792," says his biographer, Hon. Josiah Quincy, " and witnessed the assaults party spirit was making upon his early patron and constant friend, a man he so loved and respected, his indignation, heightened by the sentiment of gratitude, was irrepressible, and on April 15th he wrote Knox as follows : —

" What shall we say, my dear friend, to a certain publication, which, under the title of ' Strictures, &c.,' fabricated in Boston, is now circulating here, and no doubt has made its appearance with you ? The shameful violation of decency and truth, the virulence and rancor of his remarks on the Secretary at War, show the wickedness and malice of the author of this production in such glowing colors, as must expose him to general contempt and detestation. Happy must you feel, — thrice happy am I in the reflection, — that so long as the American name shall last, yours will be handed down with distinction in the list of the ' valued file ; ' and the artillery, which formed under your auspices equalled every exigence of war, will ever be regarded as the child of your genius. Well do I remember the honorable testimony of the gallant La Fayette amidst the thunder of our batteries on the lines at Yorktown. ' We fire,' exclaimed he, with a charming enthusiasm, ' better than the French ' (and faith we did too). To this I made a suitable objection. His reply was, — ' Upon honor, I speak the truth ; and the progress of your artillery is regarded by everybody as one of the wonders of the Revolution.' Shame, then, to this infamous scribbler! and let his heart burst under the idea that your country has derived the most substantial benefit from your services; that the good and wise acknowledge your merit; and that Humphreys was not less just than poetical in characterizing by a single line the man to whose abilities he had been witness in the various events of a long and trying war : —

> 'Ere Steuben brought the Prussian lore from far,
> And Knox created all the stores of war.' "

Under date of May 10, 1794, Knox writes to Jackson : —

. . . " I am extremely anxious that it * should be completed in the course of the year, although I have fears that I shall not be able to go there this summer. The new corps of artillery, the frigates, the fortifications, — all new business added to my former employments, together with the incessant application indispensably required by the political state of affairs in which I have more share than I am well qualified for, — form to a cloud which almost obscures my prospect of getting away in any thing like due season. I cannot leave my situation in this critical state of affairs. The services of my whole political life would serve, in the opinion of those who I esteem, in no degree to form a counterbalance to my quitting at this crisis. I therefore must stay until the storm shall have passed, or I be wrecked in the general catastrophe threatened by various causes.

" You mention the commissary of military stores. This office Mr. Hodgdon has been possessed of in a different shape for several years, and has it now. I should hope something may occur which would be agreeable to you; but my own opinion is, that neither you nor I ought to be in public life, but [should] make some exertions whereby we may better our fortunes. Whether I shall ever have

---

* Alluding to his mansion-house at Thomaston, begun in 1793, and finished the next year, at a cost of not far from $15,000. Local tradition, usually unreliable, has greatly exaggerated this, as well as other facts connected with the mansion and its occupants. For instance, it said, among other things, that the house cost $50,000; that one hundred beds were made, an ox and twenty sheep often slaughtered in a week; and that twenty saddle horses and corresponding carriages were kept to accommodate guests and sojourners.

sufficient time to lay a practical scheme for such an undertaking I cannot tell, but certainly not while I remain in public life."

Knox succeeded in procuring for his old friend the appointment of United States naval agent, and, as such, he superintended the building of the "Constitution," one of the six frigates the construction of which was ordered by the Act of 27 March, 1794.

The outrages of the pirates of the Mediterranean on the persons and property of our citizens, together with the importance of providing defences for our extensive seaboard, forcibly impressed Knox's mind with the necessity of a naval force. Jefferson and himself were the only supporters in the cabinet of the establishment of a navy, but his endeavors were at length carried into effect by his sanguine confidence in its success and his strenuous efforts for its accomplishment. The result soon vindicated the wisdom of the measure, and our navy has ever since been identified with the glory and prosperity of the country. Knox performed the duties of both departments with equal zeal and ability until the imperious claims of private interest compelled him to turn his attention to the long-neglected concerns of his family.

The expenses of his open hospitality far exceeded the limited compensation of his office, and he had for some time been determined to retire from public life. As early as in September, 1792, writing to his daughter Lucy respecting this subject, he says : —

"Having arrived, or nearly so, at the summit of human age and vigor, and being ere long to slope my down-hill course, objects appear exceedingly different to my view from what they used to do in my ascent. . . . All my life hitherto I have been pursuing illusive bubbles which burst on being grasped, and 'tis high time I should quit public life and attend to the solid interests of my family, so that they may not be left dependent on the cold hand of charity;

and in order to retire with reputation, it was indispensably necessary that I should not afford subject for calumny to feed upon, by
neglecting for a moment the services belonging to my station.   I
wish for ease, but in order to enjoy it I must make some exertions
for pecuniary objects."

The President had expressed a desire that he would remain with him till the close of his own official career, and
had from time to time induced him to continue, but at
length reluctantly accepted his resignation.   The following correspondence ensued: —

KNOX TO WASHINGTON.

"PHILADELPHIA, 28 Dec. 1794.

" SIR, — In pursuance of the verbal communications heretofore
submitted, it is with the utmost respect that I beg leave officially to
request you will please to consider that, after the last day of the
present month and year, my services as Secretary for the Department of War will cease.

" I have endeavored to place the business of the department in
such a train that my successor may without much difficulty com-
mence the duties of his station.   Any explanations or assistance
which he may require shall be cordially afforded by me.

" After having served my country nearly twenty years, the
greatest portion of which under your immediate auspices, it is with
extreme reluctance I find myself constrained to withdraw from so
honorable a situation.

" But the indispensable claims of a wife and a growing and
numerous family of children, whose sole hopes of comfortable com-
petence rest upon my life and exertions, will no longer permit me
to neglect duties so sacred.

" But, in whatever situation I shall be, I shall recollect your confidence and kindness with all the fervor and purity of affection of
which a grateful heart can be susceptible."

15

"PHILADELPHIA, Dec. 30, 1794.

"SIR, — The considerations which you have often suggested to me, and are repeated in your letter of the 28th instant, as requiring your departure from your present office, are such as to preclude the possibility of my urging your continuance in it.

"This being the case, I can only wish that it was otherwise. I cannot suffer you, however, to close your public service without uniting, with the satisfaction which must arise in your own mind from a conscious rectitude, my most perfect persuasion that you have deserved well of your country. My personal knowledge of your exertions, while it authorizes me to hold this language, justifies the sincere friendship which I have ever borne for you, and which will accompany you in every situation of life. Being, with affectionate regard,   Always yours."

Leaving Philadelphia on June 1, 1795, he visited his native town, where, on the 12th, he was invited to a public dinner by his friends and fellow-citizens. Continuing his journey, he was publicly welcomed on the 22d by the people of Thomaston, where he had fixed his future residence. He at once applied himself to the cultivation and improvement of an extensive tract of land in the then district of Maine, called the Muscongus or Waldo patent, part of which Mrs. Knox inherited from her grandfather, General Waldo, and the residue of which he had bought of the other heirs. It lay between the Kennebec and Penobscot rivers, included those of Muscongus and St. George, and comprised a large portion of what are now the counties of Lincoln, Waldo, and Penobscot. As much of this land was in the possession of squatters, it was a task of no little difficulty to quiet their pretensions; but his firm yet conciliatory course eventually overcame all obstacles. His liberality and beneficence, together with the improvements which he suggested and carried into effect, soon rendered his residence among them a blessing felt and acknowledged by all.

Prior to his removal, a splendid mansion had been erected at the head of St. George's River, having a delightful prospect in front, extending eight or ten miles down that river; and in this charming spot, to which he gave the name of Montpelier,* in the society of his wife and children, and of the distinguished visitors who from time to time enjoyed his hospitality, Knox enjoyed a larger share of happiness than he had probably ever known before. His wife, who was truly his congenial spirit, was also well satisfied to retire from scenes of gayety and fashion to the privacy of domestic life and the loved society of her children. She is described as having been, even in her latter days, when upwards of sixty, a remarkably fine-looking woman, with brilliant black eyes, and a blooming complexion. Her style of dress, which was somewhat peculiar, and her dignified manners, gave her the appearance of being taller than she really was.

"Mrs. Knox," says the Duke de la Rochefoucauld Liancourt, "is a lady of whom you conceive a still higher opinion the longer you are acquainted with her. Seeing her in Philadelphia, you think of her only as a fortunate player at whist; at her house in the country you discover that she possesses sprightliness, knowledge, a good heart, and an excellent understanding." Of her daughter (afterward Mrs. Thatcher), he says, that "at their house in Maine she lays aside her excessive timidity, and you admire alike her beauty, wit, and cheerfulness;" and of the General, "he is one of the worthiest men I have ever known: lively, agreeable; valuable equally as an excel-

* This elegant residence is no longer standing, and its site is now occupied by the station of the Knox and Lincoln Railway.

lent friend and as an engaging companion." Among his distinguished guests were Senator Bingham and his family, and several French refugees of celebrity, such as Louis Phillipe, Talleyrand, the Count de Beaumetz, and the Duke de Liancourt. The latter, whose wardrobe was replenished by the munificence of Knox, is said to have exclaimed despondingly one day while here, as he struck his forehead with his hand, "I have three dukedoms on my head, and not one whole coat on my back." Knox wrote him as follows from Boston, in July, 1797, and the duke responded by again visiting him the next September : —

"MY DEAR DUKE, — I have received with peculiar sensibility your kind letter of the 2d of this month. Under every vicissitude of human affairs I shall love and esteem you as a brother. You are not truly informed of my having a hatred for the French nation. Their great qualities of gallantry and magnanimity are above, far above, my eulogy. But as it relates to this country, they are acting under a mistaken impression of our being attached to the British nation. I hope time and better information will lessen the resentment of France against this country: it cannot be for their happiness or ours that we should quarrel. . . . I have been detained here by a variety of circumstances until this time, but more particularly in attending our legislature, who have unintentionally wronged me out of nearly 40,000 acres of my best land high up Penobscot River. I have succeeded with one branch, but could not quite succeed with the other; but I shall finish the affair next session. I shall go [to St. George's] in five days. My affairs there flourish, but want my presence there for the summer. I cannot express how delighted and charmed I should be by having the happiness of receiving you there."

Knox entered largely into brickmaking, and the manufacture of lime and lumber, and also carried on an extensive mercantile business under the management of Captain Thomas Vose, a gallant officer of artillery, at first as clerk, and afterward as partner. These and other varied industries which he carried on brought to the place and gave employment to large numbers of mechanics and other emigrants, who became permanent residents of Thomaston, and who stimulated the growth of the town. He also attempted to introduce improved breeds of cattle and sheep; and as early as 1796 undertook the business of ship-building, and several coasters were launched and kept running in his employ. To facilitate his lumber operations, Knox purchased the right to improve the navigation of George's River, and completed locks of sufficient capacity for the passage of rafts and gondolas at the several falls in Warren, opening the navigation of the river as far up as the mills in Union. His plans and projects of improvement were more suited to his expansive mind than to his actual resources, he being for the most part of the time while there greatly embarrassed by want of money; and they consequently resulted more advantageously to others than to himself. These pecuniary troubles culminated in 1798, and caused for a short time some distress to his indorsers, Generals Lincoln and Jackson, who were, however, amply secured from loss by assignments of valuable land. A few extracts from his later letters will afford some glimpses of passing events, and of his domestic life and feelings. Thus to his friend Jackson, under date of July 9, 1795, only a few days after his arrival at St. George's, he writes, "We had a small company on the 4th of July of upwards of five hundred people!" On this occasion a general invitation had been given to the people of the town and neighboring settlements to inspect the General's mansion and partake of its hospitalities. Tables were set in the piazzas, and "the house and grounds were vocal with music and conversation."

To Washington, under date of Boston, 15 January, 1797, he writes: —

. . . " The loss of two lovely children on which you condole in your letter has been recently renewed and increased by the death of our son [Washington], of seven years old. Unfortunate, indeed, have we been in the loss of eight children, requiring the exercise of our whole stock of philosophy and religion.

" We have lately come from St. George's to pass the winter in this town. Indeed, this is our general plan: we may, however, as we grow older, find it inconvenient. We are distant about two hundred miles by land, which we may easily ride in six days when the snow is on the ground; or with wheels, with a very little improvement of a small part of the road. I am beginning to experience the good effects of my residence upon my lands. I may truly say that it is more than doubled in its value since I determined to make it my home. The only inconvenience we experience is the want of society: this will probably lessen daily. Our communication by water to this town is constant and cheap. We can obtain transportation here cheaper than the same article can be carted from my store to the vessel. This egotism would require an apology to any other than you."

His last letter to Washington is dated 22d December, 1799, eight days after that illustrious man had breathed his last: —

" I am here [Thomaston], and should be more happy in my pursuits than I have ever been, were some embarrassments entirely dissipated. But this will require time. My estate with indulgence is competent, and greatly more, to the discharge of every cent I owe. All who are here unite with me in presenting to Mrs. Washington our affectionate remembrance. I may not wish you the greatest blessing by wishing you a long life, because I believe that while you continue here you are detained from a much better condition. But I pray fervently that your days on earth may be days of felicity, without clouds, sickness, or sorrow."

TO GENERAL DAVID COBB.

" MONTPELIER, 22 March, 1800.

" Returning from Boston on the 14th, I found your letter. I perceive no cause of regret at the departure of our old chief. He exhibited a most glorious setting sun ; and the people of the United States have exhibited human nature in its brilliant attitudes by their gratitude. His death and the testimonials of respect will be an excellent stimulus to future patriotism. . . .

"You mention that your spirits are not good. For God's sake bear up against the devil of Gloom. Put yourself in motion. Visit even me if you can find nothing better. Get Willich, a new author on diet and regimen ; but, above all, get — on horseback.

" I was in Boston twelve days. My affairs progress well. I shall have bright days yet. My daughter had been there for two months. She returned with me. Mrs. K. and Caroline stayed at home, which to me is, after all, the most agreeable place, provided I had you and a few other friends near me.

"Bonaparte, what a glorious fellow! how completely he has averted the monster anarchy and mad democracy ! I hope in God that no fanatic will assassinate him, which is to be dreaded."

TO MRS. KNOX AT BOSTON.

" MONTPELIER, 20 Nov. 1801.

" Whether your not getting a house is good or bad, I will not determine. With my habits, a lodging-house will be execrable, and yet feelings must give way to judgment. In either case we must be economists. Although our prospects will be greatly brightened by the revolution of our settlers, yet very little ready money at present. Therefore *prenez garde* as to expenses. Although the throng of our visitors have passed, yet we generally have eight or ten per day, and commonly from five to ten at night. Our son * is a cause of infinite solicitude. He is not here, nor have I received a line from him. At present the proposition of sending him to the East Indies or Canton appears like giving him a passport to eternity or to infinite misery."

Upon the declaration of war with France, in 1798, under the Presidency of John Adams, Washington, who was ap-

---

* Henry Jackson Knox, his only surviving son, was a midshipman in the navy in 1798–1800. He was nominated as a lieutenant by President Adams in June, 1799, but was not confirmed by the Senate.

pointed lieutenant-general, named as his seconds Hamilton, C. C. Pinckney, and Knox, in the order mentioned. The latter was greatly mortified at being placed after those who, during the war, had been his juniors in rank, and declined to serve. He wrote to Washington a remonstrance, which the latter sent to Hamilton, with a letter, delicately intimating a disposition favorable to Knox. Hamilton, in reply, reluctantly acquiesced in "any arrangement which Washington might deem for the general good;" and at a later period endeavored, in a letter to Knox, from which we make an extract, to throw the responsibility upon others. Warm-hearted and placable, Knox cherished no animosity against him, and when he heard of his death broke out into violent and uncontrollable emotion.

HAMILTON TO KNOX.

"NEW YORK, March 14, 1799.

"My judgment tells me I ought to be silent on a certain subject, but my heart advises otherwise, and my heart has always been the master of my judgment. Believe me, I have felt much pain at the idea that any circumstance personal to me should have deprived the public of your services or occasioned to you the smallest dissatisfaction. Be persuaded, also, that the views of others, not my own, have given shape to what has taken place, and that there has been a serious struggle between my respect and attachment for you and the impression of duty. This sounds, I know, like affectation, but it is nevertheless the truth. In a case in which such great public interests were concerned, it seemed to me the dictate of reason and propriety not to exercise an opinion of my own, but to leave that of others who would influence the issue to take a free course. In saying this much, my only motive is to preserve, if I may, a claim on your friendly disposition towards me, and to give you some evidence that my regard for you is unabated."

Neither the absorbing nature of his private affairs nor the pecuniary and other obstacles which constantly im-

peded his extensive plans for the improvement and settlement of the country around him, could prevent his
performance of those public duties which his fellow-citizens from time to time imposed upon him. We find him
appointed, April 6, 1796, a commissioner for the United
States for settling the Eastern boundary on the true river
St. Croix; from the year 1801 a member of the General
Court; and on June 2, 1804, he was appointed one of the
council of Governor Strong, by whom he was much consulted in important affairs, and like whom he was independent and firm in political sentiment, while at the same
time conciliatory and tolerant.

General Knox was exceedingly fond of the society of
men of learning, talent, and wit, and had an extensive
correspondence with many of the eminent men of his time
both in Europe and America. At the time of his decease
he had a handsome collection of not less than 1,585 vol-
umes, 364 of which were in the French language. Next
to that of Benjamin Vaughan, Esq., of Hallowell, his was
the largest and best private library in the district of Maine.
He received the honorary degree of Master of Arts, from
Dartmouth College, in 1793; and 16 December, 1805, was
made a Fellow of the American Academy of Arts and
Sciences.

We come now to the close of the career of this truly
noble and estimable man. Had he been permitted to attain the usual age of man, which his vigorous constitution seemed to render probable, the cloud that rested upon
the latter part of his life would undoubtedly have been
dispelled; and the rise in the value of his property would
have enabled him to realize all his anticipations, and to
have left his family in opulence. It was otherwise or-
dained. A sudden and unlooked-for accident cut him off
in the midst of his usefulness, to the sincere regret of all

16

who knew him. His neighbors mourned his loss as a public benefactor; but to his immediate family the stroke was unexpected and overwhelming.

The event occurred on Saturday, Oct. 25, 1806, after an illness of a few days. It was occasioned by his having swallowed a chicken bone, which caused a mortification, and was from its nature incurable. He was entombed on the following Tuesday with military honors, amid the largest concourse of citizens ever seen in that vicinity, and a eulogy was pronounced by the Hon. Samuel Thatcher. The House of Representatives of Massachusetts, on Jan. 10, 1807, unanimously passed resolutions of respect to his memory, which, with a letter of condolence from the speaker, Hon. Perez Morton, was sent to the widow.

Mrs. Knox died June 20, 1824. Out of twelve children, nine of whom died in childhood or infancy, only three survived their father: *Lucy F.*, b. 1776, d. 12 Oct. 1854, who m. Ebenezer Thatcher (H. U. 1798); *Henry Jackson*, b. 24 May, 1780, d. Thomaston, Me., 1830; and *Caroline*, who m., 1st, James Swan, of Dorchester; 2d, Hon. John Holmes, of Maine. Both the latter died without issue. The surviving children of Mrs. Thatcher are Admiral Henry Knox Thatcher, and Caroline F., widow of Benjamin Smith, of Newburg, N.Y.

The personal and mental characteristics of General Knox are thus described by William Sullivan in his "Familiar Letters:"—

"He was a large, full man, above middle stature; his lower limbs inclined a very little outward, so that in walking his feet were nearly parallel. His hair was short in front, standing up, and powdered and queued. His forehead was low; his face, large and full below; his eyes, rather small, gray, and brilliant. The expression of his face altogether was a very fine one.

"When moving along the street, he had an air of grandeur and self-complacency, but it wounded no man's self-love. He carried a large cane, not to aid his steps, but usually under his arm; and sometimes, when he happened to stop and engage in conversation with his accustomed ardor, his cane was used to flourish with, in aid of his eloquence. He was usually dressed in black. In the summer, he commonly carried his light silk hat in his hand when walking in the shade. When engaged in conversation, he used to unwind and replace the black silk handkerchief which he wore wrapped around his mutilated hand, but not so as to show its disfigurement.

"When thinking, he looked like one of his own heavy pieces, which would surely do execution when discharged; when speaking, his face had a noble expression, and was capable of displaying the most benignant feeling. This was the true character of his heart. His voice was strong, and no one could hear it without feeling that it had been accustomed to command. The mind of Knox was powerful, rapid, and decisive, and he could employ it continuously and effectively. His natural propensity was highly social, and no man better enjoyed a hearty laugh.

" He had a brilliant imagination, and no less brilliant modes of expression. His conceptions of the power and glory of the Creator of the universe were of an exalted character. The immortality of the soul was not with him a matter of induction, but a sentiment or fact, no more to be questioned than his own earthly existence. He said that he had through life left his bed at the dawn, and had been always a cheerful, happy man."

Says Thacher in his "Military Journal," in speaking of Knox : —

"Long will he be remembered as the ornament of every circle in which he moved, as the amiable and enlightened companion, the generous friend, the man of feeling and benevolence. His conversation was animated and cheerful, and he imparted an interest to every subject that he touched. In his gayest moments he never lost sight of dignity; he invited confidence, but repelled familiarity. His conceptions were lofty, and no man ever possessed the power of embodying his thoughts in more vigorous language: when ardently engaged, they were peculiarly bold and original, and you inevitably felt in his society that his intellect was not of the ordinary

class; yet no man was more unassuming, none more delicately alive
to the feelings of others. He had the peculiar talent of rendering
all who were with him happy in themselves, and no one ever more
feelingly enjoyed the happiness of those around him. His feelings
were strong and exquisitely tender. In the domestic circle they
shone with peculiar lustre; and if at any time a cloud overshadowed
his own spirit, he strove to prevent its influence from extending to
those that were dear to him. He was frank, generous, and sincere,
and in his intercourse with the world uniformly just."

"The conversation of General Knox," says another
writer, "was itself a feast. He was affable without
familiarity, dignified without parade, imposing without ar-
rogance."

His features were regular, his Grecian nose prominent,
his complexion florid, his hair naturally dark, and his eyes
sharp and penetrating, seldom failing to recognize a countenance they had once rested upon. His frame was well
proportioned and muscular, inclining to corpulency; and
while at West Point, in August, 1783, he weighed 280
pounds.

A firm believer in the truths of Christianity, and a liberal supporter of its institutions; he regarded the future
as a progressive state of existence, and held in slight
esteem the distinctions of creeds and sects; "for," says
Dr. Thacher, "his charity was as diffusive as the globe,
and extensive as the family of man." He could hear
others praised without envy, and delighted to enumerate
the good qualities of men in public life.

His public spirit was displayed by encouraging schools,
locating and repairing roads, promoting the erection of a
place of public religious worship, and by exciting an attention to agriculture among his neighbors. He gave the
piece of land which is now the principal cemetery in
Thomaston; a large pulpit Bible, still in use by the Con-

gregational Church there; and the first bell that ever called together the worshippers of that town, and which is still hanging in the First Baptist Church.

Of his numerous private charities we record but one. On June 23, 1797, he drew up and headed with fifty dollars a subscription for the daughters of the French admiral, Count de Grasse, who had been driven from their estates in the West Indies, and who were then in Boston in a state of destitution. It must be borne in mind that at this time he was himself in great distress for money.

We have thus sketched, briefly and imperfectly it is true, the principal events and the leading characteristics in a career well worthy the study and imitation of mankind. One of its lessons is so especially applicable to our own times, that we commend it to those of our countrymen occupying stations of public trust. It is found in the letter to his brother William (ante, p. 61), in which he says: "You know my sentiments with respect to making any thing out of the public: I *abominate the idea.* I could not [otherwise], at the end of the war, mix with my fellow-citizens with that conscious integrity, the felicity of which I often anticipate."

Many have been as courageous in the field, many as wise and patriotic in council, but few have united to these the still rarer virtues, a spotless integrity, and a noble outspoken manliness of character, in a higher degree than the subject of this brief memoir.

APPENDIX.

APPENDIX.

THE FLUCKER FAMILY.

Capt. James Flucker, of London, mariner, m. Elizabeth Luist at Charlestown, Mass., 30 May, 1717; he was taxed there from 1727 to 1756, and d. 3 Nov. 1756. She d. Sept. 1770. Their children were —

REBECCA, bapt. Charlestown, 9 Mar. 1718, m. 22 July, 1742, to Rev. John Fowle of Hingham.

THOMAS, b. Charlestown, 9 Oct. 1719.

JAMES, b. Charlestown, 23 Sept. 1721; prob. d. between 1770 and 1773.

ISAAC, b. Charlestown, 25 Jan. 1724-25.

JANE, b. Charlestown, 25 Jan. 1724-25, m. 9 May, 1758, Dr. Isaac Rand, and d. 23 Mar. 1805.

ROBERT, b. Charlestown, 26 Dec. 1727, d. 10 Oct. 1730.

ELIZABETH, b. Charlestown, 31 Dec. 1730, m. Jona. Smith of Lexington.

ANN, b. and d. 5 Jan. 1732.

Thomas, the son, last Secretary of Massachusetts Bay, was a merchant in Boston, and owned an estate on Summer Street. He was commissioned a Justice of the Peace, 14 Sept. 1756; was a member of the Council in 1761-68; a Selectman of Boston, in 1766; succeeded Andrew Oliver as Secretary, 12 Nov. 1770; was made a Mandamus Councillor, 9 Aug. 1774; left Boston for Halifax with other Tories in March, 1776; afterward went to London, where he was a member of the "Brompton Row Tory Club," — or association of Loyalists, who met weekly for conversation and a dinner, — and died there 16 Feb. 1783. His daughter Lucy (Mrs. Knox) writes to her husband on July 17, 1777: "By a letter from Mrs. Tyng to Aunt Waldo, we learn that papa enjoys his £300 a year as Secretary of the province. Droll, is it not?" In 1765, he was a member of a committee of the Council to consider and report what could be done to prevent difficulties in the proceedings of the courts of justice; and, in 1768, he assisted in drafting an address of that body to the King.

He m. 1st, 12 June, 1744, Judith, dau. of Hon. James Bowdoin; 2d,

17

14 Jan. 1751, Hannah, dau. of Gen. Samuel Waldo, who d. Dec. 1785. They had —

THOMAS, a lieut. in the British army (2d bat., 60th, at St. Augustine, in 1777), H. U. 1773; d. 1783.

HANNAH, m. 2 Nov. 1774, James Urquhart, captain 14th reg.; from whom she was divorced, and subsequently m. —— Horwood.

LUCY, b. 2 Aug. 1756 (Mrs. Knox).

Sally Flucker, who performed in Burgoyne's "Maid of the Oaks," in private theatricals given by the British officers in Boston, was a natural daughter of Thomas. She accompanied the family to England; m. Mr. Jephson, a member of the Irish Parliament, and d. early. Copley painted her portrait.

PADDOCK'S ARTILLERY COMPANY.

Prior to the organization of this company by Captain David Mason in 1768, the only military companies in Boston were "The Ancient and Honorable Artillery Company," the first regularly organized company in America, instituted in 1638; and the "Cadets," instituted about 1754, called also the "Governor's Guards," composed of the *élite* of the citizens, and forming the escort on all occasions of ceremony or commemoration. The "Train," as it was then called, was attached to the Boston regiment; and on Captain Mason's removal to New Gloucester, Me., its command passed, in 1768, to Lieut. Adino Paddock. The latter, who was a chair-maker on Common (now Tremont) Street, opposite the Granary, was a "complete artilleryman," and made of his company a celebrated military school, which furnished many excellent officers to the Revolutionary army. It was composed chiefly of mechanics, was considered equal to any that afterward entered the service; and continued to a recent period, being latterly known as the "South End" Artillery Company.

"In the fall of 1766 a company of British artillery," says Gen. Henry Burbeck, who was himself a member of Paddock's company, "bound to Quebec, was too late to enter the river St. Lawrence, and put into Boston, where they remained in the barracks at Castle William until the May following. From them Paddock's company derived instruction in the knowledge and science of field artillery. Major Paddock bought two light brass three-pounders. My father (Col. Wm. Burbeck) gave a plan or draft for the carriages, and supplied the company with every thing, such as ammunition, port-fires, and every appointment necessary for the field. I was a member of Paddock's company seven years before the war."

Paddock attached to his company as pioneers, and to man the drag-ropes, a number of German emigrants, whose uniform consisted in part of white frocks and hair caps, and who wore broadswords. The company was, for the purposes of manœuvring, divided into two sections, each taking two field-pieces, and upon such occasions went through all the evolutions of an active engagement.

" The fourth of June, 1768, being the king's birthday, was celebrated with much spirit. . . . The Governor's Troop of Guards, under Col. Phipps ; the regiment of the town, under Col. Jackson ; with the train of artillery, under Capt. Paddock,'— all mustered in King Street, where the troop and regiment fired three rounds, and the artillery responded with their new pieces." * These pieces were, on the breaking out of the Revolutionary war, kept in a gun-house at the corner of West Street. A school-house was the next building ; and a yard, enclosed with a high fence, was common to both. Paddock, who was a Tory, had expressed an intention of surrendering these guns to Governor Gage, who had begun to seize the military stores of the province and disarm the inhabitants. His design was frustrated by a few patriotic young men, among whom were Abraham Holbrook, the school-master, Nathaniel · Balch, Samuel Gore, Moses Grant, Jeremiah Gridley, and —— Whiston, who, while the attention of the sentinel stationed at the door of the gun-house was taken off by roll-call, crossed the yard, entered the building, and, removing the guns from their carriages, concealed them in the school-house, whence they were subsequently conveyed in a boat to the American lines. The guns were in actual service during the whole war ; and in 1788 General Knox, while Secretary of War, caused a suitable inscription to be placed upon them. They were named the " Hancock " and " Adams," and are now suspended in the chamber at the top of Bunker Hill Monument.

The Committee of Safety, 23 Feb. 1775, voted that Dr. Joseph Warren ascertain how many of the men who had been under Paddock's command could " be depended on to form an artillery company when the Constitutional Army of the Province should take the field, and that report be made without loss of time." In March, 1776, Major Paddock embarked for Halifax with the Royal Army ; sailed for England in June ; and from 1781 until his decease, 25 March, 1804, aged seventy-six, resided on the Isle of Jersey, where for several years he held the office of Inspector of Artillery Stores, with the rank of Captain.

The following list of members of Paddock's company is quite incomplete. Those starred were subsequently officers in the regiments of Gridley, Knox, or Crane, in the Revolutionary army : —

* Probably the brass three-pounders brought from London in the brigantine "Abigail," which arrived about Feb. 1. They had been cast for the town from two old cannon sent over by the General Court for that purpose. Upon them were engraved the arms of the Province. — *Drake's History of Boston.*

Adino Paddock, Capt. with rank of Major.
Christopher Clark,   1st Lieut.
Thomas Crafts,   ,,   ,,
Jabez Hatch,   ,,   ,,
John Sullen,   ,,
George Trott,   ,,
Thomas Bumstead,   ,,
Samuel Sellon,   2d   ,,
Edward Tuckerman,   3d   ,,
*John Crane,   private. Col.
*Ebenezer Stevens,   ,,   Lieut.-col.
*John Popkin,   ,,   ,,
*William Perkins,   ,,   Major.
*Henry Burbeck,   ,,   Captain.
*John Lillie,   ,,   ,,
*William Gridley,   ,,   ,,
*William Stevens,   ,,   ,,
*John Callender,   ,,   ,,
*David Cook,   ,,   ,,
*Thomas Seward,   ,,   ,,
*Joseph Thomas,   ,,   ,,
*Thomas Jackson,   ,,   ,,
*Thos. Waite Foster,   ,,   ,,
*Edward Crafts,   ,,   ,,
*Dimond Morton,   ,,   ,,   (brother of Hon. Perez).
*John Johnston,   ,,   ,,
*John Gridley,   ,,   Capt.-lieut.
*Jotham Horton,   ,,   ,,
*David Allen,   ,,   ,,
*Joseph Loring,   ,,   ,,
*Samuel Treat,   ,,   ,,   (killed at Fort Mifflin).
*James Hall,   ,,   ,,
*David Bryant,   ,,   ,,   (killed at Brandywine).
*John Hiwill,   ,,   Lieut.
*Thomas J. Carnes,   ,,   ,,

INSTRUCTIONS FOR HENRY KNOX, ESQ.

You are immediately to examine into the state of the artillery of this
army, and take an account of the cannon, mortars, shells, lead, and ammunition that are wanting; when you have done that, you are to proceed in the most expeditious manner to New York; there apply to the

president of the Provincial Congress, and learn of him whether Col. Reed did any thing, or left any orders respecting these things, and get him to procure such of them as can possibly be had there. The president, if he can, will have them immediately sent hither; if he cannot, you must put them in a proper channel for being transported to this camp with despatch before you leave New York. After you have procured as many of these necessaries as you can there, you must go to Major-General Schuyler and get the remainder from Ticonderoga, Crown Point, or St. John's; if it should be necessary, from Quebec, if in our hands. The want of them is so great, that no trouble or expense must be spared to obtain them. I have wrote to General Schuyler, he will give every necessary assistance, that they may be had and forwarded to this place with the utmost despatch. I have given you a warrant to the Paymaster-General of the Continental Army, for a thousand dollars, to defray the expense attending your journey and procuring these articles, an account of which you are to keep and render upon your return.

Given under my hand at head-quarters at Cambridge this 16th day of November, Annoque Domini, 1775.

G. WASHINGTON.

Endeavor to procure } what flints you can. }

AN INVENTORY OF CANNON, &c., BROUGHT FROM TICONDEROGA, DECEMBER 10, 1775, AND INSTRUCTIONS FOR THEIR TRANSPORTATION.

MORTARS AND COHORNS.

		Dim. of bore.	Ft. & ins. of length.	Weight.	Total w't.
Brass	2 Cohorns	$5\frac{7}{10}$	1—4	150	300
	4 do.	$4\frac{1}{4}$	1—1	100	400
	1 mortar.	$8\frac{1}{4}$	2—0	300	300
	1 do.	$7\frac{1}{2}$	2—0	300	300
	—				
	8				
Iron	1 do.	$6\frac{1}{2}$	1—10	600	600
	1 do.	10	3— 6	1800	1800
	1 do.	$10\frac{1}{2}$	3— 6	1800	1800
	3 do.	13	3 (average)	2300	6900
	—				
	6				

HOWITZERS.

Iron	1	8	3—4	15.2.15	15.2.15
	1	$8\frac{1}{4}$	3—4	15.2.15	15.2.15
	—				
	2 (16)				

CANNON.

Brass	8	3 pounders	$3\frac{1}{20}$	3—6	350	2800
	3	6 do.	$3\frac{7}{16}$	4—6	600	1800
	1	18 do.	$5\frac{1}{4}$	8—3	2000	2000
	1	24 do.	$5\frac{1}{12}$	5—6	16.3.18	1800
Iron	6	6 do.	$3\frac{7}{16}$	9—7	2500	15,000
	4	9 do.	$4\frac{1}{16}$	8—4	2500	10,000
	10	12 do.	$4\frac{3}{4}$	9	2800	28,000
	7 dble fortif.	18 do.	$5\frac{1}{4}$	9	4000	28,000
	3	18 do.	$5\frac{1}{2}$	11	5000	15,000

To. can., 43   total weight, 119,900
Mortars, 16

59

By all means endeavor that the heavy cannon and mortars go off first. Let the touch-holes and vents of all the mortars and cannon be turned downwards. The lead and flints are to come as far as Albany, which will serve to make up a load. Observe that 2 pairs of horses be [put] to between 2 or 3 thousand weight, and 3 or 4 pair for the 4000 weight, and 4 span for those of 5000 weight; but Mr. Schuyler the D. Q. G. will see more particularly to this affair. The one span will take above 1000 weight. They are to receive seven £ per ton for every 62 miles, or 12s. per day for each span of horses. Write to me by every slay the quantity that is upon that slay. When a number of slays go off together, one letter will serve for the whole, mentioning the cannon that each have particularly, and the people's names. All to be delivered at Springfield or Boston.

***

KNOX'S ARTILLERY REGIMENT, AS ARRANGED 16 MARCH, 1776.

Henry Knox, Col.,   com. 17 Nov. 1775.
William Burbeck, 1st Lieut.-col. ,,   1 Jan. 1776.
David Mason,   2d ,,   ,,   1 ,,   ,,
John Crane,   1st Major ,,   1 ,,   ,,
John Lamb,   2d ,,   ,,   1 ,,   ,,

CAPTAINS.

Edward Crafts.	William Perkins.	—— ——
Thomas Pierce.	Dimond Morton.	William Dana.
Thos. Waite Foster.	Stephen Badlam.	Ebenezer Stevens.
Edward Burbeck.	Eliphalet Newell.	Jotham Drury.

CAPT.-LIEUTS.

Benj. Eustis.	Jotham Horton.	John Johnston.
Wm. Treadwell.	Edward Rumney.	Thomas Seward.
Benj. Frothingham.	David Allen.	Asa Rowson.
Timothy Stow.	Winthrop Sargent.	Benajah Carpenter.

FIRST LIEUTS.

Thomas Randall.	Jona. Welch Edes.	Isaac Packard.
David Briant.	Samuel Treat.	——— ——
Henry Burbeck.	John Bryant.	David Cook.
Wm. Stevens.	——— ——	John Sluman.

SECOND LIEUTS.

Thomas Wells.	Peter King.	Thos. Machin.
John Lillie.	Joseph Savage.	Joseph Blake.
Joseph Loring.	Joseph Thomas.	John Bull.
Thos. Vose.	Samuel Shaw.	James Steel.
David Preston.	Daniel Parker.	T. J. Carnes.
Thomas Dean.	Hardy Peirce.	Samuel Doggett.
Thomas Jackson.	Isaiah Simmons.	Jeremiah Freeman.
James Furnivall.	Oliver Brown.	Jeremiah Niles.
	John Chandler.	

INTERVIEW WITH HOWE'S ADJUTANT-GENERAL.

KNOX TO HIS WIFE.

"NEW YORK, July 15, 1776.

"Lord Howe yesterday sent a flag of truce up to the city. They came within about four miles of the city, and were met by some of Col. Tupper's people, who detained them until his Excellency's pleasure should be known. Accordingly, Col. Reed and myself went down in the barge to receive the message. When we came to them, the officer, who was, I believe, captain of the Eagle man of-war, rose up and bowed, keeping his hat off: 'I have a letter, sir, from Lord Howe to Mr. Washington.' 'Sir,' says Col. Reed, 'we have no person in our army with that address.' 'Sir,' says the officer, 'will you look at the address.' He then took out of his pocket [a letter] which was thus [addressed]

" ' GEORGE WASHINGTON, Esq.,
" ' New York.
" ' HOWE.'

" ' No sir,' says Col. Reed, ' I cannot receive that letter.' ' I am very sorry,' says the officer, ' and so will be Lord Howe, that any error in the

superscription should prevent the letter being received by *General
Washington.*' 'Why, sir,' says Col. Reed, 'I must obey orders.' 'Oh,
yes, sir! you must obey orders, to be sure.' Then, after giving him a
letter from Col. Campbell to General Howe, and some other letters from
prisoners to their friends, we stood off, after having saluted and bowed
to each other. After we had got a little way, the officer put about his
barge and stood for us, and asked by what particular title he chose to
be addressed. Col. Reed said, 'You are sensible, sir, of the rank of
General Washington in our army.' 'Yes, sir, we are. I am sure my
Lord Howe will lament exceedingly this affair, as the letter is quite of a
civil nature, and not of a military one. He laments exceedingly that he
was not here a little sooner;' which we supposed to allude to the declaration of independence: upon which we bowed, and parted in the most
genteel terms imaginable."

"July 22, 1776.

"On Saturday I wrote you we had a capital flag of truce, no less than
the adjutant-general of General Howe's army. He had an interview
with General Washington at our house. The purport of his message
was in very elegant, polite strains, to endeavor to persuade General
Washington to receive a letter directed to George Washington, Esq.,
&c., &c. In the course of his talk every other word was, 'May it please
your Excellency, if your Excellency so please;' in short, no person
could pay more respect than the said adjutant-general, whose name is
Col. Paterson,* a person we do not know. He said the &c., &c. im-
plied every thing. 'It does so,' said the General, 'and any thing.' He
said Lord and General Howe lamented exceedingly that any errors in the
direction should interrupt that frequent intercourse between the two
armies which might be necessary in the course of the service. That Lord
Howe had come out with great powers. The General said he had heard
that Lord Howe had come out with very great powers to pardon, but he
had come to the wrong place: the Americans had not offended, therefore
they needed no pardon. This confused him. After a considerable deal
of talk about the good disposition of Lord and General Howe, he asked,
'Has your Excellency no particular commands with which you would
please to honor me to Lord and General Howe?' 'Nothing, sir, but
my particular compliments to both;'—a good answer. General Washington was very handsomely dressed, and made a most elegant ap-

---

* James Paterson was made lieutenant-colonel 63d foot, 15 June, 1763; colonel
in the army, 20 Aug. 1777; major-general, 10 Nov. 1782; and does not appear in
the army list after 1787. He was appointed adjutant general in America, 11 July,
1776; and was sent home with despatches after the battle of Monmouth.

pearance.   Col. Paterson appeared awe-struck, as if he was before
something supernatural.   Indeed, I don't wonder at it.   He was before
a very great man indeed.   We had a cold collation provided, in which I
lamented most exceedingly the absence of my Lucy.   The General's servants did it tolerably well, though Mr. adjutant-general disappointed us.
As it grew late, he even excused himself from drinking one glass of wine.
He said Lord Howe and General Howe would wait for him, as they were
to dine on board the Eagle man-of-war: he took his leave and went off."

DISPOSITION OF TROOPS AT NEW YORK AFTER AUG. 9, AND BEFORE THE BATTLE OF AUG. 27, 1776.

	Major-Gen. PUTNAM.	*Stations.*
Brigadiers	James Clinton (late Heath's) . .	On the North River above The Furnace.
	John M. Scott	The City.
	John Fellows	From the Glass House to Greenwich.
	Major-Gen. HEATH.	
Brigadiers	Thos. Mifflin	Mount Washington.
	George Clinton	King's Bridge.
	Major-Gen. SPENCER.	
Brigadiers	Samuel H. Parsons	From the Ship Yard to Jones's Hill, including a redoubt on the plain.
	James Wadsworth	On the East River in the city.
	Major-Gen. SULLIVAN.	
Brigadiers	Lord Stirling	As a reserve near Bay-ard's Hill.
	A. McDougall	
	Major-Gen. GREENE.	
Brigadiers	John Nixon	Long and Governor's Isl-ands.
	—— Heard	

ORDER OF MARCH TO TRENTON.

Each brigade to be furnished with two good guides.   Gen. Stephen's
brigade to form the advance party, and to have with them a detachment
of the artillery without cannon, provided with spikes and hammers to

18

spike up the enemies' cannon in case of necessity, or to bring them off
if it can be effected, the party to be provided with drag-ropes for the
purpose of dragging off the cannon. Gen. Stephen is to attack and
force the enemy's guards and seize such posts as may prevent them from
forming in the streets, and in case they are annoyed from the houses
to set them on fire. The brigades of Mercer and Lord Stirling, under
the command of Major-Gen. Greene, to support Gen. Stephen. This is
the 2d division or left wing of the army, and to march by the way of the
Pennington road.

St. Clair's, Glover's, and Sargent's brigades, under Major-Gen. Sullivan, to march by the river road. This is the first division of the army,
and to form the right wing. Lord Stirling's brigade to form the reserve
of the left wing, and Gen. St. Clair's brigade the reserve of the right
wing. These reserves to form a second line in conjunction, or a second
line to each division, as circumstances may require.

Each brigadier to make the colonels acquainted with the posts of their
respective regiments in the brigade, and the major-generals will inform
them of the posts of the brigades in the line.

Four pieces of artillery to march at the head of each column; three
pieces at the head of the second brigade of each division; and two pieces
with each of the reserves. The troops to be assembled one mile back of
McKonkey's Ferry, and as soon as it begins to grow dark the troops to
be marched to McKonkey's Ferry, and embark on board the boats in
following order under the direction of Col. Knox.

Gen. Stephen's brigade, with the detachment of artillerymen, to embark
first; Gen. Mercer's next; Lord Stirling's next; Gen. Fermoy's next,
who will march in to the rear of the second division, and file off from the
Pennington to the Princeton road in such direction that he can with the
greatest ease and safety secure the passes between Princeton and Trenton. The guides will be the best judges of this. He is to take two
pieces of artillery with him. St. Clair's, Glover's, and Sargent's brigades
to embark in order. Immediately upon their debarkation, the whole to
form and march in subdivisions from the right. The commanding officers
of regiments to observe that the divisions be equal, and that proper
officers be appointed to each. A profound silence to be enjoined, and
no man to quit his ranks on the pain of death. Each brigadier to appoint
flanking parties; the reserve brigades to appoint the rear guards of the
columns; the heads of the columns to be appointed to arrive at Trenton
at five o'clock.

Capt. Washington and Capt. T——, with a party of forty men each,
to march before the divisions and post themselves on the road about
three miles from Trenton, and make prisoners of all going in or coming
out of town.

Gen. Stephen will appoint a guard to form a chain of sentries round the landing-place at a sufficient distance from the river to permit the troops to form, this guard not to suffer any person to go in or come out, but to detain all persons who attempt either. This guard to join their brigade when the troops are all over.

LETTER TO PRESIDENT HANCOCK RESPECTING GENERAL DUCOUDRAY.

"CAMP MIDDLEBROOK, 1 July, 1777.

" SIR, — From the information I have received I am induced to believe that Congress has appointed a Mr. Ducoudray,* a French gentleman, to the command of the artillery.

" I wish to know of Congress whether this information be true : if it is, I beg the favor of a permission to retire, and that a proper certificate for that purpose be sent me immediately.

" I am, sir, your most humble servant,
" HENRY KNOX."
"Hon. JOHN HANCOCK, Esq."

DEFENCES OF THE DELAWARE, 9 AUG. 1777.

It is the opinion of the subscriber that the batteries on FORT ISLAND (Fort Mifflin) ought to have an additional work thrown up upon its left, and garrisoned with 12 pieces heavy cannon, 150 cannoneers, half as many assistants, with 500 infantry.

RED BANK to be so constructed as to have 5 or 6 cannon on the land side, and as many heavy towards the river, to prevent any ships coming up the channel leading to it, in order to flank the galleys which may be stationed for the defence of the *cheveaux de frise* near the fort.

BILLINGSPORT to be finished as at present contracted, or, if possible, more so, so as to hold 300 men, exclusive of 150 cannoneers and 75 assistants, to work 12 pieces heavy cannon, which ought to be in this work. The galleys to lie opposite to it at the head of the low island, in order

---

* This talented engineer was, on 11 Aug. 1777, appointed inspector-general, rank of major-general; and made superintendent of the works on the Delaware. While hastening as a volunteer, on 11 Sept. 1777, to the battle of Brandywine, his horse, becoming restive while on board a ferry-boat crossing the Schuylkill, plunged with him into the river, and he was drowned.

to assist the fire of Billingsport. These galleys would be for this purpose preferable to the floating batteries, as they can be most easily moved in case of an accident to Billingsport.

If much depends on the fire-ships, an enclosed battery ought to be constructed on some advantageous piece of ground near Derby's Creek, and something higher up the river than where the present defective battery is: this, in order to prevent any of the enemy's ships mooring at the mouth of the western channel, so as to prevent the fire-ships being sent round into the main ship-channel; and between this western channel is thought to be most commodious for the free operation of the fire-ships, either in the channel leading to Billingsport or further down the river. The galleys ought also to lie in the western channel if their retreat is perfectly secure, as the commodore (Hazlewood) says, as well in order to protect the fire-ships as to annoy any of the enemy's frigates which may be opposed to Billingsport. But the two floating batteries, which from their unwieldiness cannot be easily moved, together with the frigates and xebeks, ought to lie behind the second row of *cheveaux de frise* upon a line with Fort Island.

If there should be time enough, a strong enclosed work ought to be thrown up on Fort Island capable of containing 400 or 500 men, and advantage may be taken of part of the stone work already erected, and which in its present state would be infinitely detrimental to any body of men who may seek shelter from it.

These sentiments are respectfully submitted by, sir,

Your most obedient, humble servant,

HENRY KNOX,

His Excellency General WASHINGTON.   *Brigadier-Gen.*

OPINION AS TO THE FEASIBILITY OF TAKING PHILA-DELPHIA BY STORM.

In Answer to Washington's Queries, given 26 Nov. 1777.

SIR, — I exceedingly lament my want of ability and experience to fill properly the important station in which I am, and am more particularly distressed when such important questions are referred to my decision as those which your Excellency gave us in charge last evening. The happiness or misery of the people of America may be the consequence of a right or erroneous judgment.

Much has lately been urged concerning the reputation of our arms, as if we had long been a warlike nation, whose existence, like the ancient Romans, depended on their military service. I confess I view the matter differently, and cannot bring myself to believe (how much soever I may wish it) that we are upon a par in military knowledge and skill with our enemies. Indeed it is not possible, and the sensible part of mankind will know it. . . .

The gentlemen who urge the desperate measure of attacking the enemy's lines, redoubts, and the city of Philadelphia, seem to forget the many principles laid down by people experienced in the art of war against our engaging in general actions upon equal terms; against our risking our *all* on the event of single battles. In the beginning of the contest our friends in England urged the impropriety of such conduct, giving instances of numbers of States who lost their liberties by means of them. It is an invariable principle in war that it cannot be the interest at the same time of both parties to engage. It is also another fixed principle that the invaders of a country ought to bring the defenders of it to action as soon as possible. But I believe there is not a single maxim in war that will justify a number of undisciplined troops attacking an equal number of disciplined troops strongly posted in redoubts and having a strong city in their rear, such as Philadelphia.

It is proposed to attack the enemy's redoubts without being perfectly acquainted with their number, strength, or situation, with troops of whom we have had the experience of two capital actions, that it was impossible to rally them after they were broken. By the mode of attack proposed we are to stake the liberties of America on a single attempt in which the probability of success is against us, and, if defeated, of sacrificing the happiness of posterity to what is called the reputation of our arms.

It has been agreed that the enemy's force consists of 10,000 rank and file fit for duty. It is said Lord Cornwallis has taken with him from 1500 to 3000, — suppose the number 2500, which is 500 more than I believe he has, there remain 7500 rank and file fit for duty. Our returns are 8000. I say 8000, because I hold the militia in case of an attack of this kind useless entirely, for we know they will not stand within the range of a cannon-ball. We are to attack 7500 strongly posted in redoubts, having batteries and a strong city in their rear. In this instance the idea that it is necessary among disciplined troops of having three to one to storm works is laid aside, not because our troops are *better* disciplined than their enemy's, but because from a concurrence of circumstances our affairs are in a *desperate* situation, and we must retrieve them or perish.

Marshal Saxe says redoubts are the strongest and most excellent kind of field fortifications, and infinitely preferable to extended lines, because each redoubt requires a separate attack, one of which succeeding does not facilitate the reduction of the others. Charles XII., with the best troops in the world, was totally ruined in the attack of seven redoubts at Pultowa, although he succeeded in taking three of them.

The character of the British troops in Europe is far above mediocrity, and the experience we have had of their discipline and valor proves them by no means contemptible. In the commencement of this war they stormed an unfinished work on Bunker's Hill, but the experience gained there has entirely prevented them from making any similar attempts. Indeed, the Germans lately made an attempt on Red Bank, the event of which will hardly give them a favorable opinion of the attack of redoubts by storm.

The situation of the American army on Long Island, after the battle of August 27th, was exceedingly ineligible, and the enemy must have known it; but they did not attempt to carry our redoubts by storm, although, had they succeeded in one instance, and made a sufficient opening for the introduction of a large column of troops, the greatest part of our army then on the island must have fallen a sacrifice, or have been taken prisoners.

From the experience derived from reading and some little service and the knowledge of the strength of the enemy's works, my opinion is clearly, pointedly, and positively against an attack on the enemy's redoubts, because I am fully convinced a defeat would be certain and inevitable.

My opinion is to draw our whole force together, take post at, and fortify Germantown, considering it as our winter quarters. When the works there are in a tolerable state of defence, I should be for taking our whole force (except one brigade to guard the works), and proceed upon the enemy's line, offering them battle, which, if they declined, would in the opinion of every rational man fully evince our superiority in point of strength. If they should come out, fight, and defeat us, we have a secure retreat and winter quarters.

I have thus offered my sentiments to your Excellency with freedom; but if a contrary disposition should take place, and an attack be resolved upon, I shall endeavor to execute the part that may be assigned me to the utmost of my ability.

I am with the most profound respect your Excellency's most obedient, humble servant.   H. KNOX,

Brig.-Gen. Artillery.

ARTILLERY PARK, CAMP WHITEMARSH, 26th Nov. 1777.

His Excellency General WASHINGTON.

The question was, whether it would be advisable to attack the enemy's redoubts and the city of Philadelphia by way of storm; to throw twelve hundred troops into the city by the way of the Delaware, embarking them in boats at Dunx's Ferry, sixteen miles above the city.

ARRANGEMENT OF THE THIRD BATTALION OF ARTILLERY.

MORRISTOWN, 16 April, 1780.

Col. JOHN CRANE . . . . . 1 Jan. 1777.
Lieut.-Col. JOHN POPKIN . . . 15 July, 1777.
Major, WILLIAM PERKINS . . . 12 Sept. 1778.
Adjutant, JAMES GARDNER . . 1 Jan. 1777.
Paymaster, CHARLES KNOWLES . 1 Jan. 1777.
Quartermaster, SAMUEL COOPER. 9 May, 1779.
Surgeon, SAMUEL ADAMS . . . 14 May, 1778.

Captains.			1st Lieuts.		
William Treadwell	1 Jan.	1777.	Charles Knowles .	1 Aug.	1778.
Benj. Frothingham	1 Jan.	1777.	Daniel McLane .	12 Sept.	1778.
Winthrop Sargent	1 Jan.	1777.	William Price .	12 Sept.	1778.
Thomas Seward	1 Jan.	1777.	Daniel Jackson .	12 Sept.	1778.
Nathaniel Donnell	1 Jan.	1777.	Samuel Jefferds .	1 Oct.	1778.
Henry Burbeck .	12 Sept.	1777.	Florence Crowley	1 Oct.	1778.
David Cook . .	14 Mar.	1778.	Abijah Hammond	2 Dec.	1778.
John Sluman . .	12 Sept.	1778.	Joseph Driskill .	7 May,	1779.
John Lillie . .	1 Nov.	1778.	George Ingersoll	10 June,	1779.
Thomas Vose . .	2 Dec.	1778.	John Hiwill . .	22 Feb.	1780.
Thomas Jackson .	22 Feb.	1780.	Isaac Barber . .	6 Mar.	1780.
Samuel Shaw . .	12 Apr.	1780.	Thomas Bayley .	12 Apr.	1780.

Capt. Lieuts.			2d Lieuts.		
William Johnston	1 Jan.	1777.	William Andrews .	1 Feb.	1777.
Thomas Barr . .	1 Jan.	1777.	David Mason . .	1 Feb.	1777.
John Callender .	1 Jan.	1777.	John Liswell . .	1 Feb.	1777.
Isaiah Bussey . .	1 Jan.	1777.	Joseph Bliss . .	1 Feb.	1777.
John Gridley . .	1 Jan.	1777.	Samuel Cooper .	1 Feb.	1777.
John Pierce . .	12 Sept.	1778.	Samuel Bass . .	1 Feb.	1777.
John George . .	1 Oct.	1778.	Benjamin Eaton .	1 Feb.	1777.
Constant Freeman	1 Oct.	1778.	Elias Parker . .	13 Sept.	1777.
Jacob Kemper .	2 Dec.	1778.	Moses Porter . .	1 Jan.	1778.
James Gardner .	22 Feb.	1780.	William Moore .	9 Sept.	1778.
Jacob Goldthwait	6 Mar.	1780.	Edward Blake . .	10 Sept.	1778.
James Hall . .	12 Apr.	1780.			

AN ACCOUNT OF THE ORDNANCE WHICH WILL BE AT-
TACHED TO THE AMERICAN ARMY IN THE INTENDED
OPERATIONS (SIEGE OF YORKTOWN) TO THE SOUTH-
WARD.

FIELD ARTILLERY.

BRASS.

2	12	pounders.
4	3	pounders.
6	6	pounders.
3	5½	howitzers.

{ These with implements and carriages complete, and two hundred
rounds to each piece, with the
proper quantity of small stores.

15

FOR A SIEGE.

IRON.		BRASS.	
3	24 pounders.	2	8 inch mortars.
20	18 pounders.	3	8 inch howitzers.
		10	10 inch mortars.
		6	5½ inch mortars.

The above complete with carriages, beds, and implements, powder,
shot, and shells, sufficient for five hundred rounds to each piece.

H. KNOX.

PARK OF ARTILLERY, 24th August, 1781.
His Excellency General WASHINGTON.

FRENCH ARTILLERY AND ENGINEERS AT THE SIEGE
OF YORKTOWN.

ARTILLERY.

One battalion of the Royal Corps of Artillery, D'Aboville, Col. ; Nadal,
Lieut.-Col. ; 25 officers, 631 men.

ENGINEERS.

Desandrouins, Col. ; Gau, Commissary ; and ten other officers.

Siege Artillery.	*Field Artillery.*
20 24 and 16 pounders.	8 12 pounders.
4 6 and 8 in. Howitzers.	24 4 pounders.
12 8 and 12 in. Mortars.	4 6 in. Howitzers.

.

"ROUGH DRAFT [BY KNOX] OF AN ADDRESS TO HIS EXCELLENCY GEN. WASHINGTON, 14 NOV. 1783."

[*See the Farewell Address, Washington's Writings*, vol. viii. p. 491.]

" All the officers of the part of the army remaining on the banks of the Hudson have received your Excellency's Serious and Farewell Address to the Armies of the United States. We beg your acceptance of our unfeigned thanks for the communication and your affectionate professions of inviolable attachment and friendship. If your attempts to insure them the just, the promised rewards of their long, severe, and dangerous services have failed of success, we believe it has arisen from causes not in your Excellency's power to control. With extreme regret do we reflect on the occasion which called for such endeavors. But, while we thank your Excellency for these exertions in favor of the troops you have so successfully commanded, we pray it may be believed that in this sentiment our own particular interests have but a secondary place; and that even the ultimate ingratitude of the people (were that possible) would not shake the patriotism of those who suffer by it. Still with pleasing wonder and with grateful joy shall we contemplate the glorious conclusion of our labors. To that merit in the Revolution which, under the auspices of Heaven, the army have displayed, posterity will do justice; and the sons will blush whose fathers were their foes. Most gladly would we cast a veil on every act that sullies the reputation of our country. Never should the page of history be stained with its dishonor, even from our memories should the idea be erased. We lament the opposition to those salutary measures which the wisdom of the Union has planned, — measures which alone can recover and fix on a permanent basis the credit of the States, — measures which are essential to the justice, the honor, and interest of the nation. While she was giving the noblest proofs of magnanimity, with conscious pride we saw her growing fame; and, regardless of present sufferings, we looked forward to the end of our toils and dangers, to brighter scenes in prospect. There we beheld the Genius of our country dignified by sovereignty and independence, supported by Justice, and adorned with every liberal virtue. There we saw patient Husbandry fearless extend her cultured fields, and animated Commerce spread her sails to every wind that blows. There we beheld fair Science lift her head, with all the arts attending in her train. There, blest with Freedom, we saw the human mind expand ; and, throwing aside the restraints which confined us to the narrow bounds of *country*, it embraced the *World*. Such were our fond hopes ; and with such delightful prospects did they present us. Nor are we disappointed.

19

Those animating *prospects* are now changed and changing to *realities;* and actively to have contributed to their production is our pride, our glory. But JUSTICE alone can give them stability. In that JUSTICE we still believe. Still we hope that the prejudices of the misinformed will be removed, and the arts of false and selfish popularity, addressed to the feelings of avarice, defeated, or, in the worst event, the world, we hope, will mark the just distinction. We trust the disingenuousness of a few will not sully the reputation, the honor, and dignity of the great and respectable majority of the States.

"We are happy in the opportunity just presented of congratulating your Excellency on the certain conclusion of the definitive treaty of Peace. Relieved at length from long suspense, our warmest wish is to return to the bosom of our country, to resume the character of citizens; and it will be our highest ambition to become useful ones.

"To your Excellency, this great event must be peculiarly pleasing; for while at the head of her armies, urged by patriot virtues and magnanimity, you steadily persevered, under the pressure of every possible difficulty and discouragement, in the pursuit of the great objects of the war, — the freedom and safety of your country, — your heart panted for the tranquil enjoyments of peace. We cordially rejoice with you that the period of indulging them has arrived so soon. In contemplating the blessings of liberty and independence, the rich prize of eight years' hardy adventure, past sufferings will be forgotten; or, if remembered, the recollection will serve to heighten the relish of present happiness. We sincerely pray GOD this happiness may long be yours; and that when you quit the stage of human life you may receive from the UNERRING JUDGE the rewards of valor exerted to save the oppressed, of patriotism and disinterested virtue."

THANKS OF THE GOVERNOR AND COUNCIL OF NEW YORK TO KNOX AND HIS COMMAND.

CITY OF NEW YORK, Dec. 18, 1783.

STATE OF NEW YORK, ss.

In Council, &c., &c.

Resolved, That his Excellency the Governor be requested to present the thanks of this Council to Major-General Knox, and the officers and privates of the detachment under his command, for the attention they have manifested to the rights of the citizens of this State, and for their aid in preserving the peace and good order of the Southern District, since the evacuation thereof by the forces of his Britannic Majesty ; to assure them of the grateful sense this Council entertains of their essential services, as well of those that they, as a part of the American army, have rendered to the inhabitants of this State, in common with the other citizens of America during the late long and arduous contest.

JAMES M. HUGHES, Sec'y.

The above was transmitted by Governor Clinton, with the following note : —

" SIR, It gives me great pleasure to find my sentiments of the services rendered by you and the officers and men under your command to the inhabitants of this State, expressed by the Council; and it is with peculiar satisfaction that I obey their order in communicating the enclosed resolution to you, and through you to the officers and privates who are also objects of it."

LETTERS.

KNOX TO LA FAYETTE.

NEW YORK, 14th Dec. 1783.

I have written to you, my dear Marquis, several times, expressing my affection for you, and informing you how dear you were to America in general. These sentiments you must not regard as compliments, but the language of sincerity. Our independence is now established, and we feel the warmest gratitude for all the means which have contributed to effect it.

We have been flattered with the hope of your visiting us again, but in this we have not yet been gratified ; but in pursuance of the spirit which accompanied us through the war we still hope on. The English have at last left us to ourselves with the full expectation that we shall not know how to govern the ship of state, and that we must apply to the *steady and experienced pilots of Britain.* Time, which matures all things, will explain this matter.

Our much loved friend, the General, has gone from this city to Congress, and from thence to Mount Vernon, attended with the entire blessings of his country. How inexpressibly rich are his feelings ! Conscious of having done well and at the same time to have his conduct universally appreciated is a rare felicity.

I send this note by the Chevalier Villefranche, who is going with Major Rochefontaine to France. They both are men of merit and deserve the protection of all good men, therefore I am certain of their receiving your countenance.

TO LA FAYETTE.

New York, 25 July, 1787.

My dear Marquis, — I thank you for your highly esteemed favor of the 5th of May. The information is truly important [Knox here refers to the meeting of the assembly of notables], and convinces me that the French nobility possess the true spirit of justice and liberality. Go on! you are on the right road, but remember that it is rough and full of dangers. Integrity, intelligence, and perseverance will overcome, but you must neither sleep nor slumber politically. I feel so extremely interested, my dear Marquis, for your happiness, that I could not restrain the above caution: you will attribute it solely to my affection. I know your sagacity, and I also know your zeal. You have mighty difficulties to combat: dissipate them, and you attain the summit of human fame.

Our friend General Washington is anxiously engaged in the business of reforming the political machine. The Convention, in which is represented every State excepting Rhode Island, has been sitting upwards of two months, and will probably continue together for two months to come. They are secret in their councils, conceiving with great propriety that the people ought not to see only half the plan at a time. Whether the propositions of the Convention will be as useful as the occasion may require is a discovery only to be made by time. But from the characters who compose the Convention it may be fairly presumed that the result of their deliberations will be as wise as could be expected from men under the same circumstances. Many of the members without absorbing all the talents of the community are certainly men of the first abilities.

General Washington's judgment is on this great occasion, as it always has been, the effect of great deliberation and reflection. It is mature and wise. His attendance in the Convention adds, in my opinion, new lustre to his character. Secure as he was in his fame, he has again committed it to the mercy of events. Nothing but the critical situation of his country would have induced him to so hazardous a conduct; but, when its happiness is being endangered, he disregards all personal considerations.

WASHINGTON TO KNOX.

Mount Vernon, 28 Feb. 1785.

I thank you for the particular account which you have given me of the different rivers to which the British have given the name of St. Croix. I shall be much mistaken if they do not in other matters as well as this give us a good deal of trouble before we are done with them, and yet it does not appear to me that we have wisdom or national policy enough to avert the evils which are impending. How should we, when contracted ideas, local pursuits, and absurd jealousies are continually leading us from those great and fundamental principles which are characteristic of wise and powerful nations, and without which we are no more than a rope of sand and shall as easily be broken?

In the course of your literary disputes at Boston (on the one side to drink tea in company and to be social and gay, on the [other] to impose restraints which at no time even were agreeable, and in these days of more liberty and indulgence never will be submitted to), I perceived and was most interested by something which was said respecting the composition for a public walk, which also appears to be one of the exceptionable things. Now, as I am engaged in works of this kind, I would thank you if there is any art in the preparation to communicate it to me, whether designed for carriages or walking. My gardens have gravel walks (as you possibly may recollect), in the usual style, but if a better composition has been discovered for these I should gladly adopt it. The matter, however, which I wish principally to be informed in is whether your walks are designed for carriages, and, if so, how they are prepared to resist the pressure of the wheels. I am making a serpentine road to my door, and have doubts (which it may be in your power to remove) whether any thing short of solid pavement will answer."

EXTRACTS FROM KNOX'S LETTERS TO WASHINGTON RESPECTING THE FORMATION OF THE FEDERAL GOVERNMENT.

BOSTON, 31st Jan. 1785.

Your remarks on the present situation of our country are indeed too just. The different States have not only different views of the same subject, but some of them have views that sooner or later must involve the country in all the horrors of civil war. If there is any good policy which pervades generally our public measures, it is too mysterious to be comprehended by people out of the cabinet. A neglect in every State of those principles which lead to union and national greatness, an adoption of local in preference to general measures, appear to actuate the greater part of the State politicians. We are entirely destitute of those traits which should stamp us *one nation*, and the Constitution of Congress does not promise any capital alteration for the better. Great measures will not be carried in Congress so much by the propriety, utility, and necessity of the thing, but as a matter of compromise for something else, which may be evil itself, or have a tendency to evil. This perhaps is not so much the fault of the members as a defect of the confederation. Every State considers its representative in Congress not so much the legislator of the whole union as its own immediate agent or ambassador to negotiate, and to endeavor to create in Congress as great an influence as possible to favor particular views, &c. With a constitution productive of such dispositions, is it possible that the Americans can ever rival the Roman name? The operation of opening the navigation of the rivers so as to communicate with the Western States is truly noble; and, if successful, of which I hope there is not a doubt, it must be followed by the most extensively beneficial consequences, which will increase in exact proportion to the increase of the population of the country. I am pleased that you interest yourself so much in this great work.

You are so good as to ask whether General Lincoln and myself had an agreeable tour to the eastward, and whether the State societies are making moves towards obtaining charters. We went to the eastern line of this State, and found that the British had made excessive encroachments on our territories. There are three rivers in the Bay of Passamaquoddy, to which the British have within twenty years past, with a view to confound the business, given the name of St. Croix. But the ancient St. Croix is the eastern river. The British have settled and built a considerable town called St. Andrews on the middle river, which has always sustained among the people in that country the Indian name Schudac. The proper St. Croix and the Schudac are only nine miles distant at their mouths. They run into the country about sixty miles, and they diverge from each other so much, that although at their mouths they are only nine miles apart, yet at their sources they are one hundred miles distant from each other; and it is from the source the north line to the mountains is to begin. The mountains are distant from the source about 80 or 100 miles; so that the difference to this State is 100 *miles square* above the heads of the rivers and the land between the rivers, which must be 60 by 50 miles square. Our legislature have transmitted the report we made on this business to Congress and the Governor of Nova Scotia. The matter has been involved designedly by the British in such a manner that it can now be settled only by commissioners mutually appointed for that purpose. I have seen a letter from Mr. John Adams, dated last October, which mentions that the river meant by the treaty of peace was decidedly the river next to St. John's River westward; and there are plenty of proofs that the ancient St. Croix was the next to St. John's. I have been particular in this narration, that you may know the precise state of this affair, which it is probable will sooner or later occasion much conversation.

As to the Cincinnati, the objections against it are apparently removed. But I believe none have yet applied for charters. In this State it is pretty evident from communicating with the members of the legislature that we should not succeed. However, we shall attempt it previous to our next meeting in July.

(*Plan for a General Government.*)

NEW YORK, 14th Jan. 1787.

. . . Notwithstanding the contrary opinions respecting the proposed Convention, were I to presume to give my own judgment it would be in favor of the Convention, and I sincerely hope that it may be generally attended. . . . In my former letters I mentioned that men of reflection and principle were tired of the imbecilities of the present government, but I did not point out any substitute. It would be prudent to form the plan of a new house before we pull down the old one. The subject has not been sufficiently discussed as yet in public to decide precisely on the form of the edifice. It is out of all question that the foundation must be of republican principles, but so modified and wrought together that whatever shall be erected thereon should be durable and efficient. I speak entirely of the federal government, or, which would be better, *one government* instead of an association of governments. Were it possible to effect a general government of this kind, it might be constituted of an Assembly or Lower House, chosen for one, two, or three years; a Senate, chosen for five, six, or seven years; and the Executive, under the title of Governor-General, chosen by the Assembly and Senate for the term of seven years, but liable to an impeachment of the Lower House and triable by the Senate; a Judiciary, to be appointed by the Governor-General during good behavior, but impeachable by the Lower House and triable by the Senate; the laws passed by the general government to be obeyed by the local governments, and, if necessary, to be enforced by a body of armed men, to be kept for the purposes which should be designated; all national objects to be designed and executed by the general government without any reference to the local governments. This rude sketch is considered as the government of the least possible powers to preserve the confederated governments. To attempt to establish less will be to hazard the existence of republicanism, and to subject us either to a division of the European powers, or to a despotism arising from high-handed commotions.

I have thus, my dear sir, obeyed what seemed to be your desire, and given you the ideas which have presented themselves from reflection, and the opinion of others. May Heaven direct us to the best means for the dignity and happiness of the United States.

NEW YORK, 19 March, 1787.

As you have thought proper, my dear sir, to request my opinion respecting your attendance at the Convention, I shall give it with the utmost sincerity and frankness.

I imagine that your own satisfaction or chagrin, and that of your friends, will depend entirely on the result of the Convention. For I take it for granted that, however reluctantly you may acquiesce, that you will be constrained to accept of the president's chair. Hence the proceedings of the Convention will more immediately be appropriated to you than to any other person.

Were the Convention to propose only amendments and patchwork to the present defective confederation, your reputation would in a degree suffer. But, were an energetic and judicious system to be proposed with your signature, it would be a circumstance highly honorable to your fame in the judgment of the present and future ages; and doubly entitle you to the glorious republican epithet, " The Father of your Country."

But, the men generally chosen being of the first information, great reliance may be placed on the wisdom and vigor of their councils and judgments, and therefore the balance of my opinion preponderates greatly in favor of your attendance.

I am persuaded that your name has had already great influence to induce the States to come into the measure; that your attendance will be grateful and your non-attendance chagrining; that your presence would confer on the assembly a national complexion, and that it would more than any other circumstance induce a compliance to the propositions of the Convention.

I have never written to you concerning your intention of declining to accept again the presidency of the Cincinnati. I can only say that the idea afflicts me exceedingly.

That the Society was formed with pure motives you well know. In the only instance in which it has had the least political operation the effects have been truly noble. I mean in Massachusetts, where the officers are still unpaid and extremely depressed in their private circumstances, but notwithstanding which the moment the government was in danger they unanimously pledged themselves for its support, while the few wretched officers who were against government were not of the Cincinnati. The clamor and prejudice which existed against it are no more. The men who have been most against it say that the Society is the only bar to lawless ambition and dreadful anarchy to which the imbecility of government renders us so liable, and the same men express their apprehensions of your resignation.

Could I have the happiness of a private conversation with you, I think I could offer you such reasons as to induce you to suspend your decision for another period of three years. Suffer me then, my dear sir, to entreat that you would come to Philadelphia one week earlier than you would in order to attend the Convention, and to cheer the hearts of your old military friends with your presence. This would rivet their affections, and entirely remove your embarrassment in this respect of attending the Convention.

God, who knows my heart, knows that I would not solicit this step, were I of opinion that your reputation would suffer the least injury by it. I fully believe that it would not. But I believe that should you attend the Convention, and not meet the Cincinnati, that it would sorely wound your sincere friends, and please those who dare not avow themselves your enemies.

9 April, 1787.

. . . It is the general wish that you should attend. It is conceived to be highly important to the success of the propositions of the Convention. The mass of the people feel the inconveniences of the present government, and ardently wish for such alterations as would remedy them. The Convention appears the only means to effect the alterations peaceably. If that should be unattended by a proper weight of wisdom and character, so as to carry into execution its propositions, we are to look to events and force for a remedy. Were you not then to attend the Convention, slander and malice might suggest that force would be the most agreeable mode of recourse to you. When civil commotion rages, no purity of character and services, however exalted, can entirely shield from the shafts of calumny.

On the other hand, the unbounded confidence the people have in your tried patriotism and wisdom would exceedingly facilitate the adoption of any important alterations that might be proposed by a Convention of which you were a member, and, as I before hinted, President.

. . . I have a letter from the Marquis de la Fayette of the 7th of February. He looks forward to military employment in this country for the reduction of the western posts and Canada. But one might venture to predict that no such operations will be undertaken until the government shall be radically amended: at present we are all imbecility.

14th Aug. 1787.

. . . Although I frankly confess that the existence of the state governments is an insuperable evil in a national point of view, yet I do not well see how in this stage of the business they could be annihilated; and perhaps, while they continue, the frame of government could not with propriety be much higher toned than the one proposed. It is so infinitely preferable to the present constitution, and gives such a bias to a proper line of conduct in future, that I think all men anxious for a national government should zealously embrace it.

The education, genius, and habits of men on this continent are so

20

various, and of consequence their views of the same subject so different, that I am satisfied with the result of the Convention, although it is short of my wishes and of my judgment. But when I find men of the purest intentions concur in embracing a system which, on the highest delibera- tion, seems to be the best which can be obtained under present circum- stances, I am convinced of the propriety of its being strenuously supported by all those who have wished for a national republic of higher and more durable powers.

3d Oct. 1787.

. . . Every point of view in which I have been able to place the subject induces me to believe that the moment in which the Convention assembled and the result thereof are to be estimated among those fortunate circum- stances in the affairs of men which give a decided influence to the happi- ness of society for a long period of time. Hitherto every thing promises well. The new constitution is received with great joy by all the commer- cial part of the community. The people of Boston are in raptures with it as it is, but would have liked it still better had it been higher toned.

I trust in God that the foundation of a good national government is laid. A way is opened to such alterations and amendments from time to time as shall be judged necessary; and the government, being subjected to a revision by the people, will not be so liable to abuse. The first legislature ought to be the ablest and most disinterested men of the com- munity. Every well-founded objection which shall be stated in the course of the discussions on the subject should be fairly considered, and such fundamental laws enacted as would tend to obviate them.

New York, 10th Feb. 1788.

. . . The constitution has labored in Massachusetts exceedingly more than was expected. The opposition has not arisen from a consideration of the merits or demerits of the thing itself as a political machine, but from a deadly principle levelled at the existence of all government what- ever. The principle of insurgency expanded, deriving fresh strength and life from the impunity with which the rebellion of last year was suffered to escape. It is a singular circumstance that in Massachusetts the prop- erty, the ability, and the virtue of the State are almost solely in favor of the constitution. Opposed to it are the late insurgents and all those who abetted their designs, constituting four-fifths of the opposition. A few, very few indeed, well-meaning people are joined to them. The friends of the constitution in that State, without overrating their own importance, conceived that the decision of Massachusetts would most probably settle the fate of the proposition. They therefore proceeded most cautiously, and wisely debated every objection with the most guarded good nature and candor, but took no questions on the several paragraphs, and thereby prevented the establishment of parties. This conduct has been attended with the most beneficial consequences. It is now no secret that, on the opening of the Convention, a majority were prejudiced against it.

KNOX'S ESTIMATE OF HIS ANNUAL FAMILY EXPENDI-TURES IN NEW YORK, 1785, 1786, AND 1787.

(*Knox, Mrs. Knox, his brother William, four or five children, two female servants, one girl without wages, and two German boys, indented servants.*)

Daily food, averaged at 20s. York currency, per day . . .	£365	
House-rent and taxes, including £20 rent of stable . . .	215	
Keeping 2 horses, 4s. per day	73	
Repairs of carriage and harness, and shoeing horses . . .	15	
Wine	100	
24 extra dinners annually, £5 each.	120	
Servants, 2 women at $8 per month	38	8s.
2 men at the same (for clothing ind. servants) . .	38	8s.
Clothing for self and family	100	
Schooling for my children.	60	
Furniture	50	
Contingencies, including charities, subscriptions, &c. . . .	80	
Firewood	60	
	£1,314	16s.
Salary	980	
	£334	16s.

27 Aug. 1787.

HON. HARRISON GRAY OTIS'S REMINISCENCES OF KNOX.

(*Extract from a Letter to Hon. Charles S. Daveis, 3 Nov. 1845.*)

" I first became acquainted with him when I was nine years old. He then kept the 'London Bookstore' in (now) Washington Street, where Brewer & Co. now keep a large druggist establishment.* . . . The opposition of her (Miss Flucker's) family to the connection was no secret in

* No. 92 Washington Street, where the " Globe " newspaper is now published.

Boston. I learnt it in my mother's family circle, which moved in the same clique with the Fluckers at times.

" From 1801 to the end of his life, my acquaintance with him was upon the most intimate and cordial footing. . . . We were together in the legislature of Massachusetts. He did not possess the talent of debate, but was unaffectedly diffident of his oratorical powers. He was nevertheless a fluent and effective speaker. He had the gift of natural eloquence; his imagination was ardent, and his style sublimated perhaps to a fault. He often inscribed his notes upon the backs of cards; a few of which he held in his lame hand, and shuffled them over as if sorting them for a game of whist; and no man commanded more attention and respect than were willingly yielded by his auditors as a homage to his unquestioned sincerity, magnanimity, and grandeur of soul. But it was in familiar conversation with friends, and in the social, commercial, and polished circles of society that he figured to the best advantage.

" As Knox's matrimonial connection was a love-match, and both parties possessed great good sense and were proud of each other, it was understood by their friends that their mutual attachment had never waned. It was, however, well known that they frequently differed in opinion upon the current trifles of the day, and that the *iræ amantium*, though always followed by the *integratio amoris*, were not unfrequent; and that in those petty skirmishes our friend showed his generalship by a skilful retreat. On one occasion, at a very large dinner-party at their own house, the cloth having been removed, the General ordered the servants to take away also the woollen cover, which madam with an audible voice prohibited. He then instantly, addressing the whole circle, observed: ' This subject of the under cloth is the only one on which Mrs. Knox and I have differed since our marriage.' The archness and good humor of this appeal to the company were irresistible, and produced, as was intended, a general merriment."

STRICTURES UPON GENERAL KNOX.

Mr. Parton, in his paper upon Washington's cabinet in the " Atlantic Monthly " for Jan. 1873, does great injustice to the abilities of Knox.

He asserts that Knox was acquainted with only one subject (war); that he was not a man of capacious or inquisitive mind; that he was one who must take his opinions from another mind or not have any opinions; that he was in the cabinet of Washington " the giant shadow of his diminutive friend Hamilton ; " and that his original remedy for the ills of the Confederacy was to extinguish the State governments and establish an imposing general government with plenty of soldiers to enforce its decrees.

The question naturally arises, How came such a man in Washington's cabinet? Did Washington read men so badly that after a fourteen years' intimacy in camp and council, having had frequent occasion to test his capacity not only as a soldier, but as a diplomatist in conferences with the French generals and admirals; with Carleton the British commander; in allaying the discontents of the army and in disbanding it; and not only that, but having witnessed his career as War Secretary for four years preceding his presidency, — that after all this experience he could have been so egregiously deceived? How came he to retain him in a position for which, according to Mr. Parton, he was so signally unfit?

This problem admits, after all, of a simple explanation. It is found in the hostility of Mr. Jefferson to Knox, arising solely from political antagonism, and which Mr. Parton seems to have fully imbibed. This bias may still further be accounted for by a habit into which Mr. Parton has, perhaps unconsciously, fallen, of magnifying and overestimating his heroes, and by way of contrast of belittleing and depreciating the character and abilities of their political rivals or opponents. The fact that such an erroneous judgment could have been made shows conclusively the existence of a want which we have endeavored, in the present volume, in some slight degree to supply.

The letters and papers of General Knox render it evident that he was well informed not only upon military matters, but that upon such subjects as politics, finance, and government, his opinions were sought and valued by many of the best minds of the time. If Mr. Parton is right, then Rufus King, Judge Marshall, Governor Strong, Alexander Hamilton, and Washington were all wrong. As an illustration of the capacity and originality of Knox, we commend to Mr. Parton's examination his plan for a general government (*ante*, page 559). Many persons who read this paper for the first time will be surprised to learn that practically the leading outlines of this plan are embodied in our system of government; and they may also suspect that in those particulars wherein it varies from the present form, as in the length of the presidential term (seven years) and the choice of president by Congress, rather than by the present perverted electoral college system, this narrow-minded man of one idea saw nearly a century ago what we are now just beginning to see.

That Hamilton and Knox, the two Federalists in the cabinet, should generally agree, is not at all strange; nor is it strange that such agreement should occur with respect to measures to which Jefferson and his anti-federal colleague, Randolph, were hostile. That they did not always agree was evident upon the question whether the French Convention was a legitimate body, and upon the more vital subject of the establishment of a navy, upon both of which questions Knox carried his point against Hamilton's opposition. It is most certainly true that Knox, in common with the great majority of the thinking men of the time, saw and deprecated the weakness and imbecility of the Confederation, and earnestly desired a government which could make itself respected at home and abroad, and which could develop the resources of the country, and promote *national unity*. To this end he labored assiduously ; and his letters, which are replete with sound and practical views upon these great questions, furnish a sufficient refutation of such ill-considered judgments as those we have pointed out.

INDEX.

INDEX.

www.ingramcontent.com/pod-product-compliance
Lightning Source LLC
Chambersburg PA
CBHW020017030726
47500CB00002B/636

* 9 7 8 3 3 3 7 2 2 7 6 4 7 *